Prophecy of the Witch

Brionna P. McClendon

To: Jett and Iris

Brionna Paige McClendon ♡

Chapter One:
Birth

The sound of a newborn's cries filled the small room. Its squalls echoed around us. I held the blood covered baby and began to clean it. Taking a wet rag, I began to clean the baby girl's face but once the blood was wiped away it revealed a mark upon her head. My gaze moved over to the baby's parents, I wrapped the infant in a blanket and carried it over to where the mother lay. The mother reached out her arms for her child and cradled her close to her breast. The mother caught sight of the girl's mark, a distressed sigh escaped her lips.

My hand firmly gripped the young mother's shoulder. "She bears the mark of the Triple Moon Goddess. Are you aware of what that means?" I questioned the woman.

Her head nodded. "She is the prophet. The one spoken about in the prophecy." Her fingers traced over the mark, the two moons on either side of the circle. "Born on the last day of winter and first day of spring." Her auburn eyes peered up at me, "That is part of the prophecy as well, is it not?"

"The day of Ostara."

The mother sat in silence as the infant gripped her finger. Tears seemed to glisten in the woman's eyes. I shifted my gaze to meet with the father's sad, green eyes. They knew what was to come. "If someone were to find out that she is the prophet, many will hunt her down." I seated myself upon the bed next to the young woman. "Let me take her, I'll keep her safe."

The mother and father peered into one another's eyes with sorrow lacing their faces. They nodded their heads to one another. I stood from the bed and the mother handed her baby over to me reluctantly. "Keep my daughter safe." Her auburn eyes peered into the infant's face, she leaned over and placed a kiss upon the mark. "I love you, Willow."

As I was leaving the room, the baby's father stopped me. "When she is older please give this to her." He removed a silver necklace from around his neck. He opened the charm and two small pictures were encased inside. "When she wishes to know about us, give this to her."

I took the locket from him and placed it around the baby's neck. Meeting his gaze once more I said to him, "Take care of my daughter." I peered back into the room to see my daughter staring out of the window and into the dark night. She turned over in her bed facing her back to us, her shoulders trembled as she cried into her pillow.

Turning my gaze away from the room I left the cottage home, gently closing the door behind me. My hand rested upon the cedar wood door. I took a step back and retrieved my broomstick that was leaning against the cottage home. Once I was seated upon it we took flight into the night, the baby safely wrapped in my arms.

Chapter Two: Years Later

"Some have found out about the girl, Anora. You cannot hide her forever." The elder witch from the council stood before me. Her black cloak rippled along the currents of the wind. "Rumors are spreading throughout the witch community that the prophet child has been born." She lowered her hood exposing her grey hair that was pulled into a bun at the top of her head.

"You know the Exorcists will hunt her and try their best to kill her."

"Does she know of the prophecy?" Her deep brown eyes questioned me.

"She's only seven years old, how do you expect her to comprehend that?"

"You know you must tell her at some point in time. The sooner the better so she knows what her fate is to be." The elder witch sighed as she gazed down upon her wand. "I suggest that you start bringing the girl to the council hall for training. The other elders wish to see the prophet child for their own eyes as well."

My head shook, "No. Not now. Let me give her the chance of a normal, witch childhood. I don't want to throw her into all this at such a young age." I begged the woman to allow Willow a few more years of normalcy.

A sigh escaped her, "I give you nine years, Anora. We

shall speak again on her sixteenth birthday."

"I thank you, sister." I inclined my head to her.

"I still wonder why you left the coven so long ago, Anora. You were the second most powerful witch, after me of course."

"You know why, Esmerelda. Willow was placed in my care, to ensure her safety I left the coven and put the child and I into hiding."

"Ah, yes. But the child shall be brought out of hiding and then you can rejoin us if you so choose to do so."

Suddenly, the sound of a child's laughter rang in our ears. The door burst open and Willow rushed out of our small cottage home, her two cat familiars chasing after her. Her long black braid whipped through the air behind her, her straight across bangs bouncing in the wind. Those brilliant two toned emerald and auburn eyes, glistened in the sun's rays. Together, the small group ran side by side in the field of flowers. Willow's face was filled with pure, innocent happiness. She tumbled to the ground and both cats climbed upon her chest, licking Willow's face causing giggles to explode from her.

"She's growing into a beautiful girl." Esmeralda's eyes gazed upon the laughing child. Pulling her hood over her head once more she turned her back to me and began to walk away. "Nine years, Anora." With that, the elder witch climbed onto her broom and soared into the afternoon sky.

Willow ran up beside me and watched the witch fly away into the clouds. "Nana, is she a witch just like us?" The child asked in wonder as she tugged at the hem of my dress.

"Indeed she is. Now, let's go inside and get you washed up for dinner." I picked up the girl and carried her in my arms. "Come, Salem. Come, Luna." I called out to the two twin, black cats. They meowed and followed after me into the house.

Once we crossed over the threshold the door clicked shut behind us and I placed the young girl down. "Willow, go wash up for supper." The girl ran off to the bathroom with her two cats following right behind her.

I retrieved my wand from a pocket in my apron and called forth my magic. *"Oh, kitchen supplies awaken and give me your aid."* A string of light flooded from the tip of my oak wand, splitting into many thin streaks, it crawled through the air and vanished into cooking utensils. Suddenly, pots and pans came to life. Flying from cabinets and landing upon the stove top. The knobs on the stove clicked and began heating the surface of it. Grabbing a pitcher, I began to fill it with water and dumped it into the pot. With a flick of my wand the cabinet doors swung open and spice containers took flight into the air. They hovered over the pot and began to shake their contents into the boiling water. Upon one of the counters a butcher knife was set to work chopping up an onion into square bits. Once it was finished the cutting board dropped the onion pieces into the pot. The refrigerator opened and out flew cabbage leaves, immersing themselves into the boiling water. Dinner was soon to be ready. Another flick of my wand caused bowls and spoons to hover within the air next to the stove, ready for me to pour fresh soup into them. I grabbed a ladle from the drawer beside me and set to pouring soup into the bowls, once I was done they placed themselves upon the table.

"Willow, dinner is ready!" I called for the child.

Soon enough, she came dashing down the hallway and seated herself at the table. Salem and Luna brushed against my legs meowing for food. I flicked my wand causing a container of cat food to pour its contents into the cat's bowls. They rushed over and began to chow down. I seated myself at the table, Willow sat at one end waiting for me. She refused to eat until I was seated in my chair. I nodded my head to her and she began scooping a spoonful of soup into her mouth. Once it was in her mouth and touched her taste buds her eyes lit up with happiness.

"Onion and cabbage soup! My favorite!" The child exclaimed happily. She shoveled spoonful after spoonful into her mouth, devouring the soup.

I couldn't help but stare upon the girl with a sad kind of happiness. She didn't know what her fate was to be, what kind of power she hid inside of her. Though her destiny was certain her future was not. Maybe, just maybe, she could change her fate and forge a new path and life for herself. Staring upon this child before me it was hard to imagine that she could either be the savior of the witches or their ultimate demise. Many would come for her and do whatever it takes to destroy her.

For so long, the witches have been at war with the Exorcists. We've lost so many people in the battles. It was foretold in the prophecy that a young girl whom bore the mark of the Triple Moon Goddess could be the witches' savior. She could destroy the Exorcists before they destroyed us. But if they were to bless her and remove her magic from her being then they would destroy all of the witches' magic. Willow has a direct connection into the veil of magic, if her magic is removed from her and she loses that connection then the veil will be shattered.

"Nana, what's wrong?" Willow's voice broke me from my thoughts.

"Hmm? Oh, nothing my dear. Now, clean your bowl and get ready for bed."

She pulled out her black wood wand from her dress pocket, *"Oh, Dirty bowl I command you to wash yourself in the sink."* Though her wording could use a little work the bowl did as it was commanded and flew into the sink. With that, she hurried off to bed.

Later that night while Willow was sound asleep, an unsettling feeling crept over my being. Wrapping a robe around my body, I stepped out of the cottage home and looked out into the darkness of the night. I had my wand ready in hand, ready to use if needed. Then my eyes caught movement in the night sky, something was heading our way. The objects shot down to the ground a mile from the cottage. It was two Exorcists. Their white robes traveled along the breeze as they began to approach. Within one hand they held a sword with a cross shaped hilt. The other hand glowed with a holy light. Panic took over me. They had found us. I had to get Willow away from here.

"Oh, guardians of stone awaken and protect my home." The gargoyles that rested in front of the house began to move as they awakened. Their stone wings fanning out behind them, they screeched and shot forth toward the Exorcists.

Hurriedly I rushed into the cottage and into Willow's room, I awoke the sleeping child. Carrying her within my arms I ran for the back door, grabbing my broom and a basket on the way out. Salem and Luna chased after me into the field, they hopped into the basket as I leaped onto the broom. Soon, we flew into the night sky. My eyes peered back upon the fight that waged on, the gargoyles were losing. A beam of bright light blasted from one of the Exorcists hands and destroyed one of the gargoyles. Its body shattered into pieces upon the ground. Focusing ahead, I cradled the child in my arms, and set forth to find us a new place to call home.

Chapter Three:
Nine Years Later

Willow rested against the trunk of an old willow tree. Its branches swayed along the afternoon breeze. It was the eve of her sixteenth birthday. It had been nine years since Esmerelda had visited. Soon, Willow will be thrust into the witches' war against the Exorcists. Today would be her last "normal" day. Everything will change come tomorrow morning.

 Approaching her I found that she held a sketchbook within her hands. Her pencil glided across the paper as her hand guided it. I knelt beside her to see that she was drawing Salem and Luna. The cats had fallen asleep curled up together in the grass.
"You've become so talented my dear." She took after her mother. Her mother was a creative soul who loved to draw and paint.

 "Thank you, Nana. It's just a sketch for now but I was wondering if we could go into town so that I may get some new paints? I've run out of many colors." Her two toned eyes pleaded to me. She had her father's and mother's eye color.

 "Oh alright. Since tomorrow is your birthday I suppose I can get you an early gift." I ruffled her dark hair. "Go inside and get ready."

 "Thank you, Nana!" She smiled happily and rushed off into the house. Her two cat familiars had finally awoken and trailed off after the girl.

I feared taking the girl out into the town. Her birthday drew close and many have found out that the prophet child had been born. Witches and Exorcists searched for her. I've had to relocate us several times throughout the years. So many times people have come far too close to taking her away from me, I refused to allow them to do so. As long as she was in my care I would protect her with my life.

Willow burst through the front door, excitement written upon her face. She was about to seat herself on my broom but I stopped her, "There comes a point in a witch's life where they have a broom to call their own." A whistle escaped my lips and a broom flew into the sky and hovered before Willow.

"Really? I can have my own broom?" Happily, she climbed onto it and was ready to take flight into the sky.

Together we flew into the clouds, the wind whipped through our hair. Willow laughed with happiness as she zoomed through the sky. The wind blew her bangs away from her face exposing her mark. The mark of the Triple Moon Goddess. My eyes searched around us to make sure no one could see us. We were safe, for now. Soon, we found a small clearing to land in, it was a mile from the town village. We hid our brooms within the trees and set forth walking to the town. Since it was a small country town there were no cars, only horse drawn carriages passed us by. Before entering into the town I made sure that Willow's bangs covered her mark. She never questioned why it must be hidden and she never asked about her parents.

Dust kicked up in the air as we walked along the dirt road through the town. Several people passed us by, some giving us a curt nod of their head, others not even bothering to notice our existence. The less people that noticed us, the better. Soon we approached the grocery shop. We stepped up the wooden stairs and into the small store. "Willow, you may go and look for your paints." With that she scurried off to the other side of the store. While she searched the aisles I gathered up some milk and bread.

Fruits and vegetables I could grow at home with magic, so I needn't waste my money on that.

    Soon, Willow came rushing back to me with empty hands, "The store manager said they were out of paints but a store a few buildings down from here sells paints too. May I go?"

    I bit my bottom lip. I never let the child out of sight. But the store was only a few buildings down and I was almost done shopping here. With a reluctant sigh I dug into my coin pouch and gave the girl a few dollars. "Be careful, my dear."

    "Thank you, Nana!" She called out as she rushed from the store.

    Her black hair disappeared from sight.

* * *

I eyed the names of the buildings as I passed them by. Soon I came upon one that was called, *Betty's Craft Supplies*. As I pushed open the screen door a little bell dinged above my head. An older woman greeted me with a smile as I strolled down the aisles of crafting supplies. Fabrics of all sorts lined along the shelves of one of the aisles. Some were so silky to the touch while others were more rough and scratchy. Soon I came upon the paint, I found a small package of the colors I needed, with it in hand I headed to the front of the store. Once more the older woman greeted me with a smile as I approached the counter. "It'll be three-fifty."

    I handed over the four dollars that Nana had given me and grabbed the bag that held my paints from the counter. "You may keep the change." As I was leaving I waved goodbye to the woman and the screen door clicked shut behind me.

    I began my walk down the dirt road back to the store my Nana was shopping in. As I was walking a strange feeling crept along my spine. A feeling as though someone were following me. I peered over my shoulder to see a cloaked person walking behind me. I quickened my pace and ducked between two houses hiding myself behind some empty crates, my hand gripped the handle of my wand in my dress pocket. The person walked past the small alleyway and disappeared from sight. A sigh of relief escaped my lips as I stood from my hiding place. Suddenly I found myself being thrust down to the ground. My elbows scraped against the gravel. The paint I had just bought scattered across the ground around me. My hand reached for the tubes but a boot stepped on it. I forced myself to look up at the person. They wore a white robe with a hood that covered their face. They knelt down before me making themselves eye-level with me. The person lowered their hood to reveal a teenaged boy. His auburn eyes stared upon me with curiosity.

"If it's money you're looking for I don't have any." I said to him.

He didn't answer me. His hand reached out toward me and brushed away my bangs from my face. His fingers gently traced along my birthmark. His touch was gentle. Then his hand gripped my chin, titling my head up as he peered into my face. "What is your name?" The boy's voice was deep and rich.

"Willow."

He released his hold on me and stood from the ground. His boot still crushing my hand.

"What do you want from me?"

Without saying anything he turned his back to me and disappeared into a crowd of people that passed by. Quickly I gathered up my paints and rushed back to my Nana.

* * *

I watched the girl enter into the crafting store and buy paints. A smile formed on her lips as she left the store carrying a plastic bag that contained the paint she had just bought. As instructed, I followed the young witch. She caught sight of me and ducked into an alleyway. I passed by acting as though I didn't see her but I leapt up on top of the building. Once she thought she was safe she left her hiding place from behind the crates. Quietly, I leapt down from the building landing just behind her. I forced her body down to the ground, and down she fell. Her elbows scraped along the gravel as her paints flew from her bag and littered the ground. My boot covered the top of her hand as she reached for a small tube of paint. Slowly, her brilliant different colored eyes peered upon me. In her emerald and auburn gaze, I found no fear. I knelt down to the ground, my hand reached toward her face and brushed away her onyx hair. It was silky to the touch, it glided across the skin of my fingers smoothly. Behind her bangs was hidden the mark of the Triple Moon Goddess. As my finger traced along her mark I found that her skin was soft to the touch. She was the girl the prophecy spoke about. The prophet child. Here and now I could end her life. My hand forced her face to look upon me. Such a young girl was said to hold powerful magic and could destroy the Exorcists. But as I looked upon her face it was hard to imagine that she could bear such power. That she alone could destroy us. I wouldn't kill her, not now. Not until she proved to be a threat. I released my hold on her and walked away, disappearing into a crowd of people.

* * *

"My dear, what happened to you?" Willow approached me with a bag of paints held within her hand. Her elbows were bloody and covered in dirt.

"Some boy pushed me down to the ground." She shrugged her shoulders and brushed some dirt from her black dress.

"What did he look like?"

Her thin dark eyebrows knitted together as she thought. "Well at first I couldn't see his face because a white hood covered it. He followed me down the street and into an alleyway, I figured he wanted money."

Panic made its way into my heart. They have found her. Tracked us here. My eyes examined the roofs of the buildings in the town as we hurriedly rushed down the dirt road. Dust kicked up behind us because of our rushed footsteps. People gazed upon us with curious eyes as we brushed passed them. Soon we came upon the clearing and retrieved our brooms. Once we were seated upon them we soared into the sky. My eyes peered around us and examined the ground below us to make sure that we were not being followed. Willow was unaware of the danger she was in. No idea what those people would do to her. She was completely naïve to the war of the Exorcists. And for now, that's how I wanted it to be. Come tomorrow her life will change drastically.

Soon our cottage home was in sight and we landed before it. Upon our arrival Salem and Luna rushed out of the home to greet us with a chorus of meows. They brushed against Willow's legs as loud purrs escaped them. My eyes gazed upon the setting sun, night would come soon. Willow knelt down to the ground and petted her familiars lovingly. She had a big heart filled with love and I could only hope that whatever comes in the future, nothing would crush that loving heart of hers.

Once we were inside the cottage I instructed for Willow to get cleaned up for dinner. I took her black dress from her and casted a spell upon some cleaning utensils. A wash bucket was filled with soapy water and the dress soaked itself into it while a washboard set to work cleaning the dirt from it. While the girl was in the shower her familiars leapt on top of the table.

"When will we be able to talk with the girl?" Luna asked as she licked her paw.

"Yes, I would like to know as well. We have been her familiars since she was a child." Salem chimed in.

"Wait until tomorrow, once she knows everything."

"But it is normal for familiars and their witches to speak with one another, besides we would never tell her of the prophecy." Luna said.

"I cannot risk a slip up. If one of you were to bring it up on accident, then she would be thrust into the war sooner."

"That is understandable but tomorrow is her birthday and on that day she shall know all." Salem stated in a matter-of-factly tone of voice.

"Then it shouldn't bother you to wait one more day."

Once the washboard had finished cleaning the dirt from Willow's dress, it floated out the back door and clothespins clipped it to a wire so that it may dry. Soon footsteps sounded down the hallway as Willow approached the kitchen. Her onyx hair was damp and fell down the length of her back, stopping at her waist. She had brushed her bangs back away from her eyes exposing the mark of the Triple Moon Goddess.

"Nana, could you trim my bangs for me?" She asked as she seated herself down upon a wooden chair.

"You can enchant a pair of scissors to do that for you, my dear."

"I know but I like it when you cut my hair." Her eyes begged to me.

"Oh, alright." I grabbed a pair of scissors from a nearby drawer and set to work trimming her bangs. Thin black hairs scattered across Willow's white dress. "Why have you not asked about your parents?" I questioned her.

She was silent for a moment before saying, "I figured you would tell me when you felt I should know."

"Would you like to know of them now?" I questioned the young girl.

"Please."

Once I had finished trimming her bangs I disappeared from the kitchen and into my room. I retrieved the silver locket from my jewelry box that her father had given to me. Holding it against my chest I returned to the kitchen and seated myself at the table. Gently, I placed the locket upon the table before the girl.

Her eyes stared in wonder upon the necklace. Her hands reached for it and her fingers popped open the locket. There she found a picture of her father on one side and a picture of her mother on the other side. Her finger traced across the surface of her mother's picture. A smile tugged at her lips. My hand placed itself upon the girl's arm.

"You look exactly like your mother." I said to her.

"Will I ever be able to meet them?" Her voice whispered softly.

"Maybe someday."

"Nana, may I keep this necklace?" Her emerald-auburn eyes gazed upon me as her fingers wrapped around the necklace.

I stood from the table and placed a kissed upon the crown of Willow's head. "Of course, my dear. Now, get to bed. It's late."

The young girl smiled as she placed the necklace around her neck. Calling for her cats she walked down the hallway toward her room and tucked herself into bed. Later that night when she was sound asleep I stood at her doorway. As she slept she appeared so innocent. It was hard to believe that she had such strong magic. That she was the prophet. My heart ached with sadness at the thought of tomorrow.

Chapter Four:
The last day of Winter and the first day of Spring

It was the day of Willow's sixteenth birthday. The last day of winter and the first day of spring. The day of Ostara. Esmerelda would be paying us a visit sometime within the day. Nine years have passed by since her last visit. Now it was time for Willow to know what she is and what she is destined to do. A yawn echoed down the hallway as Willow entered into the kitchen rubbing the sleepiness from her eyes. She seated herself at the table and stretched out her aching muscles.

I sat a plate of freshly baked food before her. "Happy birthday, my dear." I placed a kiss upon her brow and brushed some stray hair behind her ear.

"Thank you, Nana." The girl set to eating her scrambled eggs, toast, and bacon. Once the plate was licked clean she drank her milk in one gulp. Willow held her black wand within her hand, *"Oh, dishes of mess rise and cleanse yourselves in the sink."* Doing as they were commanded the plate and cup flew into the air and landed in the sink. The faucet poured hot water onto the dishes and a scrubber set to work cleaning the food off the plate.

Willow's gaze peered out the open window. A warm spring breeze swept across the field and crept into the house. The

sky was cloudless as the sun shined brightly over the land.
"Nana, is it alright if I paint outside?"

"Of course, change out of your bed clothes and you may."

With that, she rushed off into her room. She returned wearing a dark green, short sleeved crop top and a long brown skirt that flooded across the floor. In her arms she held her sketchbook and paints. She rushed outside to her usual spot under the old willow tree. She ducked under the low hanging branches and seated herself against the tree's trunk.

I was seated at the kitchen table, a warm cup of coffee held between my hands. Anxiously my fingers tapped on the sides of the mug as my eyes stared upon the clock. It ticked as its hands slowly made its way around the circle. It was early in the morning and I had no clue as to when Esmerelda would make her arrival.

Several hours passed by and I wondered outside to check on Willow to see how her painting was coming along. There she sat beneath the tree, her hand busy at work. I seated myself beside her and peered at her sketchbook. The painting depicted the cottage we called home with each of us in the painting. Willow was seated upon her broom with Luna resting on her lap and Salem leaping up onto the back of the broom. I was standing beside her with my arm snaked around the girl's shoulders. Bright, happy smiles were painted across our faces.

"This painting belongs in a frame."

"I wanted to make a painting so we could remember our time here. We're always moving and never stay in one place for very long, so I wanted to remember it." She placed the wet painting down on the grass before her then she grasped her wand and called forth her magic. *"Oh, wind of nature I summon you forth."* She directed her wand to her painting and a gust of wind breezed past it, drying it instantly.

When we stood to enter back into our home my eyes caught movement within the sky. Down the person fell from the clouds and landed in the center of the field. The person's black robe rippled along the breeze of the wind as they stepped onto the ground off their broom. The person lowered their hood to reveal grey hair and a woman's face.

Willow nudged my arm with her elbow, "Nana, who is that woman?"

Before I could answer the person did for me. "My name is Esmerelda young witch. I'm from the witch's council."

"Willow, go inside and brew some tea for our guest." The young girl scurried off into the cottage.

"As promised, I gave you nine years. It is time now for her to know of the prophecy." Her hawk like brown eyes stared upon me.

"I know, Esmerelda." I began to lead her toward my home.

"You still have not informed her have you?" One of her eyebrows raised as she questioned me.

"I have not."

Once we were inside the cottage Esmerelda seated herself at the kitchen table. Willow set before the elder witch a steaming cup of freshly brewed tea and set one before me as well. Esmerelda took a sip of tea and nodded her head in satisfaction. Her cup clinked against the saucer as she set it down upon it. The elder witch cleared her throat before she spoke. "Willow, please take a seat." As instructed the girl sat herself down at the table and waited for the woman to continue. "I am here today to inform you of a prophecy." Nervousness took over my mind as the witch began to speak.

"A prophecy was foretold over five hundred years ago that a young witch would be born with the mark of the Triple Moon Goddess. This witch would either by the savior of the witches or their downfall. The witch was said to have a direct link into the veil of magic and if she were to be blessed by an Exorcist then the veil of magic would be shattered. It is also said that the witch could put an end to the Exorcists."

Willow stared upon the elder witch with curious emerald-auburn eyes. "Why are you telling me of this prophecy?"

"Because my dear Willow, you are the witch that the prophecy speaks about."

The young witch's eyes widened with shock as she shook her head. "No, you must have me confused with another."

Esmerelda stood from the table and approached the girl. Holding her wand in her hand she used it to brush away Willow's bangs, exposing her mark. The elder witch placed the tip of her wand upon the mark. "This is the mark of the Triple Moon Goddess. You are the prophet that is spoken of in the prophecy."

Willow stood from her chair, "Nana have you known about this all along?" The girl questioned to me with pleading eyes.

My gaze fell to the brown liquid within the cup that was set before me. I couldn't bring myself to look the girl in the eye. "Yes."

"All this time, why didn't you tell me?"

"Because I wanted to give you the most normal childhood I could."

My words seemed to ease Willow's anger and confusion. She fell back into her chair and sat there quietly sorting through her thoughts. Esmerelda placed her hand upon the girl's shoulder. "That is not the only reason why I've come here today." Willow peered up at the woman. "I need for you to come back with me to the witch's council hall. There we can teach you in magic and keep you safe from harm."

"I'm used to moving anyways." Willow stood from the table and walked off into her room where she began to pack her bags.

Esmerelda seated herself next to me and placed her hand over mine. "If you wish, you may come with us as well. Maybe even rejoin the council."

"I'll come with you but I am not joining the council. Not again."

I stepped away from the table and began to prepare my belongings for departure.

* * *

Turning around I gazed back upon the cottage house. The place I had learned to call home for three years. Now, I was leaving it behind to venture forth to the witch's council hall. Salem and Luna's soft fur brushed against my legs as they meowed to me. Both of them leaped into the air and seated themselves on my shoulders.

"Finally, we can speak with you Willow. We've wanted to so desperately for so many years now." When an older woman's voice sounded from Luna I was taken back with shock.

"Y-You can talk?"

"Not just Luna but me as well." Salem's deep voice chimed in.

Both cats purred into my ears as they rubbed their faces against my cheeks. "Oh, we are so happy we can finally speak with you, Willow. It's not natural for a witch's familiar to not speak with them." Luna said as she licked her paw.

"Willow, come. It's time to leave." Esmerelda called out to me from her broom. Nana hovering beside her.

Taking one last glance back at the cottage home I leapt onto my broom and joined Nana and Esmerelda in the sky. We soared through the clouds as we followed behind the elder witch. We flew over cities and towns. The day slowly turned into night. The setting sun casted shadows over the land and turned the sky into shades of red and orange. My hands gripped the broom stick tightly until my knuckles turned white. Anxiety ate away at me as I thought of the prophecy. Was I supposed to fight these Exorcists people? Is this what my life was going to be from now on? I looked upon my two cat familiars. They have always been by my side since childhood. They nudged their cool noses against my face, reassuring me that everything was going to be okay.

Later on, we landed before a massive building. The stone was black drenching the structure in darkness, hiding it away during the night. Crimson streaks shot through the stone like lightning. Onyx marble stairs led up toward two massive wooden doors. Black metal knobs shaped in the style of gargoyle heads had loop handles hanging from their open mouths. Large cathedral like windows were placed along the side of the building, the glass within them was stained in dark colors. Stone pillars lined along the edge of the structure. It seemed to be like a castle. It was truly magnificent. Gargoyles rested upon the roof, two were stationed at the beginning of the stairs, and others were set atop the stone pillars. Their duty was to guard this place and the witches inside.

We stepped off our brooms and followed Esmerelda toward the stairs. She stood before us and stretched out her arms wide. "Welcome to your new home."

Chapter Five:
Our New Home

Once we entered into the council hall my eyes took in the view before me. A long crimson carpet stretched out across the enormous room. The floors, wall, and ceiling were completely black. Stone pillars lined down the center of the room. Aged old paintings decorated the dark walls. Crimson curtains looped across the ceiling and hung down in two rows of fabric points. Two gargoyle statues were positioned beside the massive doors. A large chandelier hung down in the center of the room bathing it in an orange glow.

Salem and Luna leapt down from my shoulders and landed upon the black marble floor with soft thuds. Nana stood beside me with her bags in hand. This was to be our new home for a while, perhaps forever. Suddenly, I was really beginning to miss our cottage home.

"The other elders wish to see you. Leave your bags at the door, I'll have someone carry them up to your rooms." Esmerelda led us down the crimson carpet and veered off to the right down a long and narrow hallway. Smaller chandeliers lined across the ceiling coating the hall in a golden, warm glow. At the end of the hallway were two more large oak doors. Cat head shaped doorknobs had handles hanging from their open mouths. Esmerelda's hand wrapped themselves around the handles and pulled the doors open. Once we entered into the massive room I found that the elder witches were already waiting for us. Raised up on a stone slate they were seated at a large stone table that hid the bottom portion of their bodies. My eyes only found their torsos. Esmerelda stepped forth onto crimson circle of stone in the marble floor and withdrew her wand from her robe.

"Oh, elders of times past I stand before you with greetings and news. Present to me the powers of your wands." Each of the elders sang in unison. The tips of their wands radiated a circular light that pulsated into the air. Each of their lights formed together and exploded into glittering magic that flickered through the air and died out as it reached the floor.

"Sister Esmerelda. What is your news?" An older man with blonde hair combed to the side addressed the witch that stood before him.

"I have brought the prophet child with me." She turned her brown eyes upon me and motioned for me to join her. Nana urged me forward with a push of her hand. I stood beside the elder witch and my eyes gazed upon the other elders before me.

The witch with blonde hair directed his attention toward me. "Please, brush aside your bangs so that we may see the mark for our own eyes." At his request my fingers pushed back my black bangs exposing the mark upon my forehead.

Gasps and whispered murmurs spread throughout the twelve people seated at the table. Some leaned and whispered into one another's ears while others just made eye contact or hand gestures toward me. A few of them just raised curious eyebrows as their gazes locked upon me. I had a sickening feeling in my stomach and all I wanted was to go back to our cottage home and forget about the prophecy.

"We cannot allow her to run freely while she contains the power to destroy the veil. She must be kept here and never again is she to leave these walls." A woman voiced her thoughts of what to do with me. I could feel the shame weighing down on me in her piercing blue gaze.

"Keep the girl locked away so that she can grow a hatred toward us? Is that such a wise idea, sister Nehemiah?" Another woman questioned the elder witch. Her eyes were much kinder when they gazed upon me. The woman appeared to be so young. Her brunet hair fell in curls down past her breasts and her green eyes peered in wonder upon me.

Once more the witch man spoke up, "Sister Arya is right, Nehemiah. Locking the girl away in shame is no way to treat her."

"Or we could put an end to the young witch's life. We wouldn't need to fear of the Exorcists blessing her and shattering the veil of magic. We could end it all right now." A man with midnight black hair that was slicked back into a long ponytail stared upon me in disgust. His hawk like features were harsh and his black eyes were filled with hatred. His finger nails clicked against the stone table.

"We could end it all right now, you are right brother Darrio. But killing an innocent is not what we do here." The blonde haired man spoke against Darrio's words.

"We could end the life of one innocent and save the lives of thousands, brother Artemis."

Artemis stood from his chair and directed his attention to me. "Young witch, what is your name?"

"Willow." My voice was hushed.

"And what do you do in your spare time?" I found his question to be rather odd.

"I draw and paint, elder Artemis." I said shyly.

"A love for the arts huh? Would you happen to have a piece of your work with you?"

I glanced back at Nana, our bags were at the entrance doors to the building. She nodded her head and quickly rushed off down the hallway. Her footsteps echoing behind her. A few moments later she returned carrying in her grasp a rolled up piece of paper. She handed it over to me and returned to her spot by the doors. I directed my attention back to the golden haired witch.

"Please present to the witch's council your work."

Carefully I unrolled the paper and held up the painting I had finished earlier today. The painting that depicted our home, Nana, my cat familiars, and I. The elder smiled at my work and nodded his head.

"A lovely painting." He turned his attention to the rest of the council. "A pure and innocent soul, Willow is of no threat to us. So, to those of you who look upon her in shame, you are in the wrong. We will not end her life to ease the fear in your minds. We will train her well and she will be our savior."

Sister Arya smiled and nodded her approval, as did many others among the council. But Nehemiah's sharp blue eyes stabbed into me like daggers. Darrio's blacker than coal eyes wished for one thing, my death. Those two I had a feeling I would need to keep my eyes on while I stayed here. Esmerelda led us from the council room and up a staircase that led to the second level of the building. She guided us to a door near the end of a hallway and unlocked it for us. Within the room there was a small living room with a red velvet couch set before an unlit fireplace. Two tall windows took up the majority of one wall, thick red curtains draped over them. A crimson oval carpet stretched out upon the blackened floor. There were three other doors within the room. Two of them led to bedrooms while the other one led to a bathroom. We found that our bags had been placed in our separate rooms.

"I'll be back for you in the morning. Your training shall begin." Esmerelda shut the door behind her as she left us alone in our room.

I tossed my body upon the velvet couch as an exhausted sigh escaped my lips. My hand rubbed my forehead where the mark of the goddess was. Maybe if I rubbed hard enough it would go away, but I knew it wouldn't. This was my life now. I was the witch the prophecy spoke of. And now, I had council elders wishing to end my life and Exorcists wanting to "bless" me. A groan rose in my throat as my hands pressed against my temples. Salem and Luna leapt onto my lap and nudged their faces against my hands, moving them away from the sides of my head.

"Do not think too much of the prophecy. Go and get some sleep. You have a busy day ahead of you tomorrow." Luna spoke to me.

Without arguing I moved from the couch and entered into my new room, the new place I called home. My body fell onto the plushness of the bed and seemed to melt into the mattress. The two cat familiars curled up beside me and together we drifted away into the land of dreams.

* * *

The following morning I had awaken earlier than I wanted too but I couldn't force myself back to sleep no matter how hard I tried. Groaning, I rolled out of bed and quietly left my room making my way across the living room and into our bathroom. When I clicked on the lights I was nearly blinded by their brightness. I ran a brush through my long, thick midnight hair and washed away my morning breath as I brushed my teeth. Before leaving the bathroom I quickly relieved myself and returned to my room. I searched through my bags trying to find a decent outfit to wear during my training today. I pulled out a lacey, floor length, black skirt and a matching lace crop top to go along with it. After dressing myself I returned to the bathroom and scattered several small braids throughout my hair.

In the living room I peered upon the clock that hung upon the wall, eight o'clock on the dot. Once I slid on my black roman sandals there was gentle knocking upon our door. Before I approached the door my hands tapped my sides, searching my pockets to find that my wand was not on me. My sandals slid across the marble floor as I rushed to my room and retrieved my black wood wand from my nightstand. Then I approached the door and swung it open to find Elder Arya standing before the threshold. Her mossy green eyes gazed upon me as a smile formed upon her sweet lips. Her brunet hair was pulled up into a high ponytail that fell in bouncy curls down to her lower back. Two thin pieces of hair framed around her heart shaped face.

"Greetings, Savior Willow." She held out her black wand before me and the tip of it was ignited in a sphere of light.

My brow raised in question to the witch. "Why did you call me savior?"

She didn't lower her wand, "Because *you*, Willow, could save the witches from destruction. You and you alone are the only who can save us."

A sigh escaped me as I raised my wand in the air, "Greetings, Elder Arya."

The tip of my wand glowed brightly and the spheres of light lifted themselves into the air and swirled around each other above our heads. Then they collided causing an explosion of magical glittering lights to flutter around us in all sorts of radiating colors. Elder Arya smiled happily and led me down the hallway and down the staircase into the entry room. Veering off to the left I followed her down a winding, dark staircase. White candles floated within the air down the hall with small flames flickering upon the candle's wicks. We were bathed in a warm light as we traveled down the halls. Half of Arya's face was cast in a dark shadow giving her a look that almost seemed menacing. Such a sweet face could turn so evil in just the shadows from the light. She was no helpless woman, that much I knew. She was an Elder and there was telling what she was capable of or what sort of things hid away deep inside her past. A chill crept down my spine, like someone's fingers trailed down the bare skin of my back. My body shuddered. The black cloak that covered her body didn't ease my mind either. From what happened yesterday with Elder Nehemiah and Elder Darrio, I wouldn't come to trust people here so easily.

Soon, we found ourselves standing before a door that was labeled *Scholar Room*. Arya turned the dark metal of the knob and thrust the door open with a creak. The room was dark until we stepped over the threshold. Flames lit upon the wicks of candles that floated through the air around the room, seeming to have a mind of their own. The room smelled of aged old books that you would find in small vintage shops in country side villages and towns. An oval polished wooden table sat at the far side of the room, four chairs circled around it. On the other side of the room lined three bookshelves across the wall. They were each overflowing with books. Elder Arya walked to the crimson circular carpet that was stretched out across the floor and seated herself upon it. Her legs folded under her as she sat up straight waiting for me to join her.

"Elder Esmerelda has instructed me to teach you in magic."

"What sort of magic will you be teaching me today?"

"Today, I am going to teach you to see the veil of magic. Other witches, including us Elders cannot see it. But you, Willow, you can."

"But if you can't see it, how do you plan on teaching me to see it?" My question came out more rude than I meant for it too.

"For many years, you have lived a sheltered life. You haven't unlocked your true power in magic, as of now I can see that at least half of it lays dormant inside of you."

"And you want to help me unlock the other half?"

A sigh escaped her, "Since it has laid dormant for so long, it'll take time for it to awaken."

"So, what do you want me to do now?"

"Now, I ask of you to close your eyes."

I did as she asked and closed my eyes, listening to the sound of her voice.

"Focus on the magic that burns inside of you like a warm fire. Now, I want you to search for your connection to the veil. Find the line of it and allow your soul to follow it to the veil."

Her voice guided me. I felt the magic inside of me burning like a great flame, crackling and sizzling through my veins wildly. I could almost feel the burn of it, a warm sensation crawled along my skin. Then, I found it. A silver glittering line. My soul seemed to attach to it and glided along it till an explosion of light enveloped my being. I had found my connection to the veil. When I opened my eyes, all around me I could see shimmers of light, glitters of magic that were as colorful as an oil slick. Everything was bathed in a heavenly white glow. When my gaze landed upon the Elder before me I could see the magic in her body. The streams of light that swam through her veins. Her magic was powerful. I could tell by how brightly it burned. A strand of silver light expanded from her body and wisped into the air above her. Her connection to the veil of magic, that is where her and every other witch's power streamed from. My hand reached toward it but something inside of me screamed stop. My fingers hovered before her connection to the veil. If I touched it, then her magic would be shattered. I lowered my hand back into my lap. All around me I could sense magic. The magic that stemmed from the candles to help guide them into the air. I could feel the magic pulsating from Elder Arya's being.

"You have found your connection." Arya whispered.

"Everything is so bright and iridescent. I can see and feel the magic around me."

"You can block your sense to all of that if you focus hard enough."

Closing my eyes, I focused on closing off my senses to the veil. Though I could no longer see the magic around me I could still feel it, and I knew that my connection to the veil was still attached to my soul. I could feel it.

"Elder Arya, I thought I was the only witch with a connection to the veil? When I entered into it I could see a thin line of connection coming from your body."

"You are the only one who can enter into it. The only one

with a direct connection. All witches power stems from the veil but none of us can see it. None except you. And since you have that connection, if an Exorcist were to bless you with their purification power then their power would stream into your line of connection straight into the veil. And once their purification enters into it, then it shatters."

"When I was in the veil and saw your connection, I reached out for it but something inside of me told me to stop. Can I sever other witches connection from the veil?"

"Yes." She answered me with stern eyes. "If you are not careful you can severe the link between a witch and their magic."

"Yesterday, in the council room Elder Darrio wished for me to be killed. Would that not destroy the veil?"

"No. Only if an Exorcists purifies you." She leaned toward me, "That is why you must be wary about the people around you. Many witches will fear you, others will shame you, but most of all some will want to kill you."

I met my gaze with hers as one of my eyebrows raised. "Even wary about the people in the room with me right now?"

A sweet smile formed on her lips, "Come, it's time for breakfast."

* * *

Elder Arya showed me the way to the dining room. She excused herself once we stood before the doors to the room. Wrapping my hands around the loop handles I swung the massive doors open to reveal a large room. Three rectangular tables stretched across the enormous room and many people were scattered in random places at the tables. Groups sat together eating and chatting away while others would seat themselves away from the chattering groups and ate alone in silence. Men and woman pushed carts of food into the room and pushed them against the wall, replacing the half empty carts with fresh food. The scent of greasy bacon, eggs, waffles, toast, and melted butter filtered through my nose. But one scent stuck out the most amongst the other smells of food. *Coffee.* I approached the carts and began to pile my plate with fresh foods, as I was reaching for a fork my hand brushed against another person's hand.

"I'm sorry…" I mumbled as my eyes moved to gaze upon the person that stood before me. There stood a girl, seeming to be my age. Her hair was fiery red and reached down to her shoulders in short waves. Her complexion was pale with freckles scattered across her cheeks and the bridge of her nose. Her dark brown eyes gazed upon me with annoyance. Her gaze slid down my body and a smirk formed upon her bright red lips.

"Hippie much? Maybe you should stop shopping at thrift stores and throw away those out dated, old clothes." Her words were sharp and took me by surprise. I hadn't done anything to this girl except accidentally bump her hand.

Before I could answer, another girl approached us. Her long, straight, almost white hair was parted down the center of her head. She placed her hands upon her well curved hips and stared down the girl (or should I say, stared up to the girl?) that dissed my clothes. "Why don't you take your prissy, stuck up attitude somewhere else, Danielle?"

"Scurry away little mouse, I'm sure your family of rodents is looking for you." Danielle sneered as she walked away, flipping her short red hair over her shoulder.

The white haired girl sighed as she shook her head. Then she turned her crystal clear blue eyes to me. "I'm sorry you had the unfortunate pleasure of meeting the Queen B."

Though Nana was not a cursing woman I had been in enough towns to know what Queen B meant. The short girl reached out her small dainty hand to me, "But you do have the fortunate pleasure of meeting me. Hi, my name is Snow."

Her name struck me as odd but I shook her outstretched hand. Her skin was so soft. "My name is Willow. Nice to meet you."

"And for the record, I happen to like your style. It's different, unique." She smiled brightly revealing a row of perfectly straight white teeth. "You're new here, I've never seen you around before. Unless I'm just that oblivious to everything that's going on around me."

"I just moved in yesterday."

The girl raised a white eyebrow to me. "Are you related to one of the Elders or workers here?"

"No." I answered her.

"No one is allowed to live here unless they're related to an Elder or worker. What is so special about you?" Her arms crossed over her chest as she peered upon me curiously.

I didn't know if I was allowed to speak of the prophecy or not. Was I supposed to keep that hidden? Or was I allowed to speak freely about it? Snow's face lit up with realization as she gasped. "You're the one the Elders have been talking about! You're the prophet child I heard my mother talking about!"

"Who's your mother?"

A sigh escaped her bubblegum colored lips. "Nehemiah. I think my mother is wrong about you. At least, now that I've met you myself."

"But you hardly know me."

"I have time and enough curiosity to kill all nine lives of a cat." She shrugged her shoulders. "So, how about I learn a little bit about you tonight. Meet me outside in the garden at eight?"

"Uh, sure." This girl was odd but I had a feeling that we would get along great.

"Alright, see you then new girl!" She called out over her shoulder as she walked away, swaying her hips.

* * *

Once I had finished my breakfast I fixed up a plate for Nana and headed back to our room. When I entered Salem and Luna rushed out of my bedroom and brushed their soft fur against my legs, meowing their greetings to me. Breaking a piece of bacon into two pieces I gave them to the cats. They chowed down on the greasy meat happily. Nana was sitting on the velvet red couch knitting a baby blue colored scarf. I seated myself beside her and handed over the plate of fresh breakfast food. She smiled and took the plate from my hands.

"How was your morning? I heard Elder Arya taught you in magic today, how was that?" Nana asked me between bites of food.

"She helped me find my connection to the veil. Everything was so strange, bright, and colorful. I could see and sense all of the magic around me. Even now when I've blocked off some of my senses, I can still feel the magic spilling out of your being."

She took a drink of orange juice and placed the cup and plate onto the table beside the couch. "From this point forward, your life will change drastically, Willow." She placed her aged hand on top of mine.

"I know, Nana." My eyes wondered over to the half kitted scarf. "Winter is over, why are you knitting that?"

She chuckled as she resumed knitting the blue yarn together. "It's the only hobby I have and being in here alone all day does get rather boring."

"Salem and Luna don't keep you company?" I gestured over to the two snoozing cats curled up on the crimson carpet.

Nana and I exchanged giggled laughter and she resumed her knitting. Excusing myself from the small living room, I returned to my bedroom. My bags lay upon the floor as did most of my clothes that I had dug through earlier this morning. I peered around the room and decided to unpack my bags, I was going to be living here for a long time and we wouldn't be returning to our cottage home anytime soon. It was time to unpack my bags and settle into my new life. I neatly folded my clothes and placed them in drawers. The dresser was crafted from cherry wood and polished. Taking my bags, I tossed them into the corner of my closet. The only things left to put away now were my art supplies. Tubes of paint, brushes, palettes, and paper lay scattered upon my bed. My gaze wondered over to the clock that rested upon my night stand. In red numbers it said eleven thirty. Eight was so far away it seemed and as far as I knew, I had no other plans for the remainder of the day. My hands scooped up my art supplies and lay them across the surface of the cherry wood desk. Pulling out the chair I seated myself upon the black velvet cushion and set to work painting.

    Several hours passed by and an almost finished painting lay before me. A dark building contrasted against the white background of the white paper. Later I would fill in the background with old oaks without their leaves and a dark night sky to go along with the creepy feeling of the painting. I stood from my desk and entered into the living room, Nana was nowhere to be found. Her bedroom door was closed and I assumed she was taking a late afternoon nap. Salem and Luna yawned and stretched out their long bodies across the floor and skipped toward me. Kneeling down I scratched the cats on top of their heads and approached the large cathedral windows. Pushing back the crimson curtains my eyes gazed upon the orange evening sky. My stomach growled with hunger and I wondered what time dinner would be served.

    Suddenly, Nana's door creaked open and out she stepped into the living room. "Willow, it's almost time for dinner." She said reading my mind. She buttoned up her dark purple cardigan and straightened her slacks as she headed for the door.

    With that, I followed her out of the room, trailed by Salem and Luna. The cats leapt onto my shoulders as we wondered down the hall and descended down the stairs. The smell of cooked foods wafted into the air around us and filtered into my nose. My mouth began to water and my stomach growled loudly.

My familiars meowed as they too smelled the fresh food. We entered into the large dining room and I found that many people filled the room, surprising me since earlier this morning it was nearly empty with a few scattered groups of people. Carts of food were lined against the walls, Nana and I fell into line and waited for our turn to make our plates. Slowly, the line advanced forward and we fell into step behind everyone. As we stood there I had the feeling of someone staring two burning holes into my back. I didn't have to turn around to know who it was that stood behind me.

"Hello again, Hippie Witch." Danielle said in a mocking tone.

I ignored her comment and made my plate, then following Nana over to one of the long wooden tables. We seated ourselves at the very end away from everyone else. I shredded up pieces of chicken and made a pile of it on the table. Salem and Luna chowed down on the chicken bits happily. As we ate another person joined us, sitting down next to me. The girl's snow-white hair was pulled into a messy bun at the top of her head and her blue eyes beamed happily as she greeted me. "Hey, Willow."

"Hey, Snow." I greeted her with a smile.

"Already made a friend?" Nana asked curiously.

"I have. Nana this is Snow. Snow, this is my Nana." I introduced them to each other.

"It's a pleasure to meet you, daughter of Elder Nehemiah." Nana said.

"How did you know who my mother was?" Snow asked curiously with her head cocked to the side.

"An old woman like me knows more than you think." She chuckled. "Plus, you favor her quite a bit, young witch."

"Ah, yes. The white hair and blue eyes are a dead giveaway." She sighed dramatically.

A faint squeak sounded into my ears as a white mouse popped its head out of the pocket in Snow's black cardigan. The creature crawled across her shoulders and sniffed the air around me, its beady red eyes stared into mine. It squeaked once more and nudged its face against Snow's pale cheek. "Willow, meet my familiar, Frost."

Such wintery names these two had. The mouse peered at me once more, "It is an absolute pleasure to meet you, Marked Daughter of the Goddess." The creature spoke in such a formal tone with a slight hint of a British accent.

And yet, another odd name I was being called. Was this something else I had to get used to as well? "It's a pleasure to meet you as well, Frost."

The mouse scurried down her arm and approached my familiars who had finished eating their chicken. At first I feared that the cats would attack the mouse but thankfully that didn't happen. Instead, they had a rather formal conversation as they introduced themselves to one another. Once we were finished with our food we stood to return to our room.

"Still meeting tonight at eight?" Snow asked with her mouse familiar perched on her shoulder.

"In the garden, right?"

She smiled brightly, "Right!"

Chapter Six:
Meeting in the Garden

Black metal fencing lined along the exterior of the garden. Sharpened points rose into the sky from the blackened metal. Approaching the gate, I unlatched it and slowly pulled it open, a creak sounded through my ears as the metal was moved. I entered into the garden and shut the gate door behind me. What lay before my eyes was a massive fountain set in the center of the garden, marble benches circled around it. A stone path led toward the fountain and into other areas of the vast garden. Rose bushes lined along the edges of the path, newly bloomed roses filled the air with a sweet scent. My fingertips trailed across the silky crimson petals of the flowers as I made my way toward the fountain. The sound of running water filled my ears. Water cascaded down the circular levels of the fountain and into the bottom pond-like part of it. Water spurted from the top of the fountain and into the air. Lily pads floated across the top of the crystal clear water, water lilies blossomed atop of the green pads.

    I seated myself upon the cool marble bench and waited for Snow to join me in the garden. As I waited my eyes wondered around peering at everything before me, taking in the sight of this beautiful place. Fireflies danced within the air like golden lights. The sound of the frogs sang through the quiet night. I found myself to be completely at peace in this place. It had a calming effect on my being. Someday soon I would need to come back here and paint the scenery so I would never forget the beauty of this place.

Then, the sound of the gate creaking open sounded in my ears. I peered over my shoulder to find Snow approaching me. Her long, white hair glowed in the moonlight as it swayed behind her in the wind. Perched upon her shoulder was her mouse familiar, Frost. Snow took a seat beside me on the bench and smiled warmly. Frost squeaked a greeting to me and crawled onto the girl's lap.

"Good evening, Willow. Glad to see you didn't change your mind." Her long, thin fingers rubbed the mouse's back while it was curled into a ball on her lap.

"So, what would you like to know about me? That is the reason you asked for me to meet you here."

"Hmmm… What could I ask you?" She pondered for a moment, her white brows knitting together as she thought of a list of questions to ask me. Her fingers snapped together, "Are you talented in anything other than magic?"

"What makes you think I'm talented in magic? For all you know I could be the worst witch ever."

"Well, you are the prophet child so it's kind of a given that you're talented in magic." She placed a hand on her hip, "Now, answer my question."

"Well, I enjoy painting. Besides that, there isn't much else I'm talented in unless you count me reading books in my spare time a talent."

Her blue eyes widened as her hands clapped together happily. "You're a painter?! May I see one of your paintings, please?" She begged with big puppy-dog eyes.

A giggle escaped from me as Snow was filled with excitement. "Of course, maybe tomorrow if I'm not busy?"

"Tomorrow it is then." She smiled. "Now, you can ask me a question."

"Well, how long have you lived here?" I couldn't think of much else to ask her.

"Since I was a baby this place has been my home. Not

many people my age live here besides Queen B so it gets a little lonely." She peered down at her familiar who was sound asleep in her lap. A soft, sad kind of smile formed on her lips. "If it wasn't for Frost, I wouldn't have any friends." Then her blue gaze turned to me, "But now, I also have you."

Not knowing what to say I smiled back to the girl. At first I was terrified of leaving my cottage home and moving to a place that would be so new to me. I feared I wouldn't make any friends but now, that fear was gone. I had Snow and I knew that we would get along perfectly.

"Speaking of the Queen B, whose daughter is she?" I asked curiously.

Snow's blue eyes rolled, "Elder Darrio is her father. They look nothing alike but damn does she look exactly like her mother. The only thing she inherited from her father is her nasty attitude. I swear those two are like two peas in a pod."

"Is her mother an Elder as well?"

"No, she's one of the kitchen staff and not a very talented witch. Honestly I don't know what that woman sees in Elder Darrio, man gives me the creeps and he's an ass."

I recalled his comment he made when I was first brought before the witch's council. "When I first arrived here, he wanted me to be killed. Saying that if they ended my life they would be saving the lives of thousands." My hands gripped the edge of the marble bench until my knuckles turned white.

"And I guess my mother was in agreement with him?"

"She wished for me to be locked away here and never allowed to leave again."

A sigh escaped from Snow's bubblegum pink lips. "I'm nothing like my mother…" Her words were a faint whisper as they drifted along the breeze. Pain weaved itself in her crystal blue eyes as she stared upon the stone ground.

Placing my hand upon her shoulder I asked, "Are you alright?"

Her eyes snapped away from the ground and a reassuring smile appeared on her lips. "Yeah, just tired is all. My mother instructs me in magic and her lessons last all day."

"Why do her lessons last so long?"

"Because someday I am to replace my mother on the witch's council so she wants me to be prepared and to be as strong as I can be."

"Do all of the Elder's children replace them on the council?"

"Someday, could be any day. That is why she is hard on her lessons, any day I could replace her and she wants me to be prepared." While saying this she had a distant, saddening look in her gorgeous eyes.

"Snow, is that what you want to do? Be on the council in the place of your mother?"

"It's not about what I want. It's the rule, the law we go by. The eldest child of an Elder steps up and takes their place when the parent is too sick to do their duty or is dead."

"I'm sorry, Snow." I didn't know what else to say. There was so much I had to learn. Rules and laws that I had to abide by.

"Well tonight you learned more about me than I learned about you." She chuckled lightly.

"I guess I did. Is there any other questions you would like to ask me?"

Her blue eyes gazed curiously at my forehead. "May I see it? The mark of the goddess?"

My fingers swept aside my dark bangs to reveal the mark that tattooed my forehead. Snow's hand reached toward my face and her fingers gently traced over my skin. "Two crescent moons attached to either side of the full moon." She said in an awe struck voice. I could feel as her cool fingers trace over the lines of the moons, her touch was gentle and careful. Quickly her hand snapped back, "Oh, I'm sorry. I shouldn't have touched you without asking." She apologized embarrassed.

"No, don't apologize, it's okay." I smiled reassuringly to her.

Then Snow leaned in close to my face, focusing hard. Her eyes narrowed. "I didn't notice your eyes before. One green and one brown. That's amazing."

"Well, thank you. My Nana said that I inherited one color from my father and the other from my mother."

Her head cocked to the side causing her white hair to sweep down over her shoulder and onto her lap. "Do you not know your parents?" A hint of sadness and pity echoed in her voice.

I turned my head away from her avoiding the pity that glazed her eyes. Instead I focused my gaze onto the stone ground. "No but Nana said that I will probably meet them someday. When? I have no clue." My hand reached toward my neck and my fingers wrapped around the silver locket that contained the pictures of my parents. The only thing I had of them.

"I can kind of understand how you feel. I've never met my father, my mother said he left before I was born." I couldn't bring my eyes to meet with hers but I knew she stared upon me. "Well, I suppose it's getting late." Finally, I brought my gaze over to her. Her brilliant blue eyes stared up into the dark night sky. Frost stretched out his sleeping limbs and scurried up her arm to perch on her shoulder.

Snow stood to leave and turned back to me, "Are you not coming inside?"

"Um, not yet. I'll stay out here for a bit longer."

"Alright, good night Willow." She smiled.

"Good night, Marked Daughter of the Goddess." Frost squeaked in his formal, British accent. The two of them walked off together and disappeared into the darkness of the night. Soon, I was alone with my thoughts and the sounds the night brought. I leaned my head back and gazed upon the vastness of the night sky. Thousands of stars twinkled across the blackened sky and the moon was full and bright. I much preferred the night over the day. Everything was calm and quiet. The world seemed to be fast asleep in its dreamland.

Though I thought I was alone I had this creeping feeling that someone was watching me from a distance. My senses were on alert. I grasped the handle of my wand in my hand and stood from the bench. Holding my wand before me I turned in circle from where I was standing. My eyes glided across the area searching for someone. My skin prickled and the hair on my arms stood on end. Something was drawing me toward the fence that circled around the garden. I found myself approaching the fence at the far end of the garden. My eyes squinted as I tried to see through the darkness of the night. *"Oh, light of light come to me and grant me sight."*

The tip of my wand ignited in a sphere of holy light. Now, I could see more clearly. My gaze wondered across the empty field on the other side of the fence, nothing appeared to be there but my eyes landed upon the silhouette of a cloaked figure. "Who are you?" I questioned the mysterious person.

They said nothing, only approaching the fence closer. I took a step back as the person came dangerously close. Their white cloak rippled along the breeze of the wind that swept by us. An air of mystery shrouded this person. Who were they? A sense of familiarity flickered like a candle flame inside of me. The person's hands reached toward their hood and pulled it down. Once more I found myself staring into those auburn colored eyes. They were rich and deep with color. Golden flecks seemed to dance around his pupils. "You were the guy from the town."

He cocked his head to the side, in doing so it caused his dark brown hair to fall into his eyes. He took me in, staring upon me with curiosity. The only words he spoke to me where asking me of my name, I remembered the deep and rich sound of his voice. But now, he spoke nothing. Not a single word escaped his lips. This person had followed me, tracked me down. But why? What did he want? Who was he?

"What do you want from me?" I demanded to know.

"Nothing, for now." He turned his back to me and raised his hood back over his head. "We will meet again, Willow." With that, he walked into the darkness of the night and disappeared from sight.

Chapter Seven: Encounter with Elder Darrio

After I informed the Elders of what happened at the garden everyone has been on alert. Gargoyles circled the sky around the council hall during the day and night. Doors and windows were sealed and locked after eight o'clock. For the time being no one was allowed out after curfew. Once the doors were locked no one was getting in and no one was getting out. Though many people did not agree with this, I for one felt safer.

I found out that the boy was an Exorcist. But if they wanted me dead, or blessed, or whatever, then why didn't he harm me? Through both of our encounters he asked of my name and said that we would meet again. The only time he actually laid his hands on me was when he shoved me down to the ground. Which I thought was highly unnecessary.

Elder Arya returned to fetch me for morning teachings in magic. Once more I followed her down to the scholar room. When we entered into the room the candles were lit with flames as they floated through the air above our heads. Elder Arya seated herself at the table and motioned for me to join her. After I set before her she retrieved her wand from a pocket hidden in the inside of her cloak. Pointing it toward the bookcases she said, *"Oh, books of knowledge come and teach me what you know."*

Saying this, a few books removed themselves from the shelves and hovered through the air toward us. Two plunked down on the table with soft thuds while Elder Arya caught one within her hand. In her grasp she held a red leather bound book that had golden lettering upon the cover of it. A golden rectangle framed around the outer edge of the book. Elder Arya flipped open the book and skimmed through the thin, aged pages. "Now Willow, do you know any of the witch's laws?"

I scrambled through my brain for a moment. "Not to use magic around humans or in public places?" I said as more of a question than a statement.

She nodded her head, "That would be one of the laws. You also cannot cast magic against humans. Anything else you know?" Her emerald eyes never looked up from the book.

"Snow told me that if an Elder falls ill or dies than their child steps up and takes their place."

That caused her eyes to gaze up from the book. "Yes, that is true and one of the oldest laws we still follow." She closed the book and plopped it on the table. "I took my father's place on the council after he fell deathly ill. I'm one of the youngest council members in history, so far."

Elder Arya did appear to be younger than the other council members. Her face was near flawless and porcelain like a doll. Her cheekbones were high and sharp, her nose was slim and short. The shape of her face was that of a heart, what many people called the perfect face. Grey hairs did not dare grow through her brunet locks. The look in her emerald eyes was cunning, mischievous, and wise. Wise beyond her years it seemed.

"How old are you?"

A wicked grin spread across her lips, "What do you suppose my age is?"

"You can't be much older than me. I say twenty-three?"

She chuckled, "Close, but no. I'm twenty-one. I had just celebrated my birthday the day before you arrived here." She straightened herself in the chair, regaining her proper posture. "Now, we have strayed far off the subject of conversation. Willow, can you tell me why we don't cast spells in front or against humans?"

All witches knew the answer to this, we've had a terrible and dark past with the humans. "The Salem Witch trials. Humans feared us and thought of us as Satan's demons, so they burned and killed many of our kind. So, to this day we are careful to not use magic before human eyes. In doing so, we keep our kind safe from harm or suspicion."

"I see your grandmother taught you well of our history."

"She didn't want me to be completely blind to the witch world and its history."

We were suddenly interrupted when a woman entered into the room. I couldn't help but admire her exotic beauty. Her skin was a smooth milk chocolate color. Her onyx hair was thick and curly, falling a little bit past her shoulders. Her eyes were a rich auburn color with golden ringlets around her pupils.

"Greetings, Elder Enya." Elder Arya stood from the table to greet the woman. Her wand was held before her with a sphere of light radiating from the tip of it.

"Greetings, Elder Arya." The woman pulled out a wand that looked like it had been crafted from a tree root. A sphere of light ignited on the tip of her wand.

The two spheres of light lifted off from their wands and circled around each other within the air above them. Then they collided, sparkles buzzed through the air, and glittering wisps of magic fluttered down to the ground and vanished.

"I've come to fetch you, Esmerelda wishes to speak with you about the prophet child." Her auburn eyes glanced over to me and smiled formed on her cherry red coated lips.

"Alright, I'll pay her a visit in just a moment."

Elder Enya nodded her head and left the room. Elder Arya turned her attention back to me. "Before I leave, do you have any questions?"

"Why do you greet others with spheres of magic?"

"Only Elders greet each other in such a way. It's a way for us to show our magic, the power of it can be rated from the brightness of our spheres and the way it reacts to another Elder's sphere. In doing this we can see which one of the two Elders could over power the other. It's like a way of showing dominance I suppose."

"But the other day, you greeted me in this way."

"Yes, because you deserve the same respect as any Elder and it was a way for me to see how far advanced you are in magic." She grasped my shoulders and looked me deep in the eyes. "One day you will surpass every Elder and witch. All you have to do is unlock the rest of your powers."

She released her hold on me and left the room. The books upon the table lifted into the air and returned themselves to their spots on the bookcases. Seeing no point in remaining here I left the room as well. As I was wondering the halls I accidentally bumped into someone. I stumbled backward and almost fell to the ground but a hand gripped around my forearm and stopped me from falling. I glanced up to apologize to the person I bumped into and who I saw before me was Elder Darrio. My heart sank in my chest as I stared into his black eyes. He loosened his grip on me with a look of disgust on his face. I broke my gaze away from his and peered down at the crimson carpeted ground.

"I'm sorry…"

"If you were paying attention to your surroundings then this would not have happened."

I coward under his scrutinizing glare. He was being harsher than needed. But what else did I expect from the man that wished for me to be killed? Elder Arya warned me to be wary of everyone, even the people on the witch's council.

"You are correct to be wary of me." His words caused me to look up at him. "I'm allowing you a chance to prove to me that you are worthy of living. Prove to me that you are not a threat to the witches. But if you fail to prove yourself then I will not hesitate to end your life myself."

His words struck fear into my very soul. A cold chill crept along my spine. His face was casted in shadows, a faint glow from a candle nearby barely lit up one side of his face. He leaned down closer to me. "Do I make myself clear, *prophet child*?" He spit out those last words with disgust like they tasted foul in his mouth.

"Yes, Elder Darrio."

He regained his posture and brushed past me as he began to walk away. But he stopped in his tracks. "Do not disappoint me, Willow. I rarely give out chances such as this. Prove yourself." It seemed as though he actually did want me to live and to prove to him, prove to everyone that I could save the witches.

I watched him leave with mixed emotions bubbling inside of me. His black cloak rippled behind him as he disappeared down the hallway.

"Willow!" A familiar voice called out my name.

I turned around to see Snow walking toward me with a smile upon her face as she waved. Frost was perched on her shoulder like usual. His beady red eyes stared into mine as he nodded his head in greeting. "Why are you just standing in the hall?"

I gazed back in the direction where Elder Darrio had disappeared. "No reason, just wondering around."

"Well you promised to show me some of your paintings if you weren't busy today."

"I just finished my lesson with Elder Arya. Follow me." I led her through the hallway up the staircase to my Nana and I's room. The door creaked open and Salem and Luna came rushing toward us, meowing their greetings. Their soft fur brushed against my legs as I entered into the room. Nana wasn't in her usual spot on the couch so I figured she was in her room.

Following me into my room Snow seated herself on my bed. Frost scurried down her arm and greeted my feline familiars.

"Here's one I've just started working on." I held out my unfinished painting to Snow.

She gripped the paper in her hands and stared upon it with amazement. "You're painting the Council Hall, it looks so realistic!" Her fingers glided across the painted building. "Oh, you can paint pictures of the celebrations that take place here!"

"Celebrations?" I seated myself beside her on the bed.

"We celebrate the holidays of the witches. Our next biggest holiday is Samhain but that's months away from now."

"My Nana and I would celebrate the holidays together, but nothing big or fancy."

"Well celebrations here are definitely *big* and *fancy*." She emphasized those words.

Handing me back my painting I laid it out across my desk so that I may work on it later. Then I seated myself in the chair and faced the girl that sat on my bed. Frost and my familiars had scurried off into the living room leaving Snow and I alone.

"So, why were you just wondering the halls?" She asked.

"I had just finished my lesson with Elder Arya and didn't know what else to do, I was wondering around due to boredom and curiosity. But I accidentally ran into Elder Darrio."

"Did he do anything to you?" Worry was written across her pale face.

"He said that he was giving me a chance to prove myself worthy of living and if I failed then he would kill me." I propped my elbow up on the back of the chair, rested my head on my hand, and peered out the window. "But as he was leaving he told me not to disappoint him and basically said he wanted me to prove myself."

Snow shook her head, not seeming to understand his words. "Elder Darrio is a complicated and confusing man, I'll give him that."

Frost, Salem, and Luna rushed back into my room. The white mouse leapt onto my bed and crawled up Snow's arm to rest on her shoulder. Salem and Luna jumped onto my lap. "It's time for dinner!" They meowed with hunger.

Scooping the cats into my arms I began to leave the room, followed by Snow and Frost. Once more the dining hall was filled with many people. The tables were almost completely full, luckily Snow and I were able to find two seats at the beginning of the long table. This time many of the witches brought their familiars along with them. Ravens flew through the air, snakes slithered around their witch's shoulders, cats meowed, mice and rats scurried around underneath the tables. It was loud with laughter and tableside conversations. Everything seemed to be okay and I was enjoying my meal and talking to Snow until a familiar, prissy voice sounded behind me.

"Figures that two weirdos like you would become friends. The little rodent has expanded her small family." Danielle stood there with a snide look on her face. Her fiery hair was tied into a bun at the top of her head and she wore a dress that showed off way too much of her figure.

"Ah, look the Queen B is gracing us with her," Snow's gaze glided down Danielle's body and a chuckle escaped her, "ever so *conservative* presence."

The sly smirk on Danielle's face disappeared. "I was gifted with an amazing body so I have every right to show it off." Then she walked over to Snow and leaned down close to her face, "And I'm sure that Erin enjoys the view."

Snow glared back into Danielle's face, her brows creasing together in anger. Danielle had struck a nerve and she knew it, like she enjoyed taunting Snow. "Piss off, she-demon." Snow practically spat the words in Danielle's face.

"Later, freak shows." She winked a brown eye at us and left, her hips swinging from side to side. I thought she would pop a hip out of place if she swung them any faster. A raven swooped down from the ceiling and perched on her shoulders as she left the dining hall.

"Bitch." Snow muttered under her breath. Frost scurried up to her and she ran her fingers across the mouse's white fur, she seemed to calm down as she petted her familiar.

"Uh, who is Erin?"

She sighed, "A witch guy that lives here that's our age." The look in her eyes told me that she had feelings for this boy.

"I'm sensing that there's more you aren't telling me."

"Is that your goddess given powers telling you that?"

"Nope, your face is giving away what you're thinking."

"Well, he's the only guy here our age and Danielle has formed some sort of competition in her mind between her and I. And the prize is Erin. But she doesn't seem like his type, he's quiet and stays mostly to himself."

"Whereas, Danielle is stuck up and bitchy?" I asked.

"Yup, they wouldn't be a good match for each other." She propped her head on her hand and stared off into space.

"Which Elder is his parent?"

Her blue gaze found its way to my face, "Elder Arya is his older sister. Their parents died a few years ago."

"She told me during a lesson that her father fell deathly ill and she took his place on the council." I pushed my food around on the plate, picking at it with my fork.

"The life of a child born from an Elder. That is all we have to look forward too." There was a hint of sadness in Snow's voice. She stared blankly upon her uneaten food.

"Snow, you must eat." Frost nudged her hand. "It is my duty as your familiar to make sure that you are healthy and your wellbeing is taken care of." He squeaked in his British accent.

"I know." Snow ran her fingers across the mouse's back and picked up her fork.

Once dinner was over Snow and I parted ways and returned to our own rooms for the night. I worried about her, she hadn't eaten much of her food and her mood had changed drastically. She wasn't her normal self after her little disagreement with Danielle. When I entered into the room I saw Nana sitting upon the couch. "Good evening, Willow."

"Hey, Nana." I smiled to her as I sat down on a red cushioned chair.

"How was your day my dear?" She reached out and held my hand in hers.

"My lesson with Elder Arya didn't last long today but afterward I ran into Elder Darrio in the hallway." Her grip on my hand tightened at the mention of the man's name.

"Did he say or do anything to you?" She eyed me carefully.

"He told me that he was giving me a chance to live and prove myself worthy and if I failed then he would kill me." Her nails dug into my skin. "Nana, you're hurting me."

She released my hand and broke her gaze away from mine. "I'm sorry, Willow." Then she leaned toward me, her eyes narrow. "Stay away from Elder Darrio and never find yourself alone with him."

"Okay, Nana." It shocked me to see her act in such a way. I had never seen her like this before.

Luna leaped from Nana's lap as she stood from the couch and walked toward her room. "Goodnight, Willow." She said before shutting the door.

Chapter Eight: Blood Witches

"Now for today's lesson, you'll learn that not all witches are good and don't worship the goddess." Elder Arya was seated before me on the crimson carpet.

"Bad witches?" I asked her.

"The witches that stray away from the path of light are called Blood Witches. Can you take a guess as to what magic they call forth?"

"From their name I can guess it has something to do with blood. Maybe taking the life of other things?"

"Close, very close Willow. They make sacrifices to the dead in order to draw forth magic from the other world. The world of the dead. The one's who turn away from the path of light and travel the one of darkness very rarely and sometimes never return to the light."

"What would make a witch decide to travel the path to darkness?"

A sigh escaped Elder Arya, "Many things. Death, revenge, passion, anger, heartbreak. A witch's powers are connected to their feelings. When a witch is angry and casts magic it goes berserk. They have no power over it once it's unleashed. And in that moment of unclear thoughts and over powering emotions is when a witch makes their decision. Now, not every time a witch loses control means that they'll choose darkness. Sometimes even in a sane state of mind witches choose to convert."

"How can you tell a blood witch from a regular witch?"

"Their eyes will be crimson like blood but many hide their eye color with magic to prevent people from knowing. But you can see and sense the magic in a witch. You will be able to tell the difference when you enter into the veil."

"Is a blood witch's magic the same as a regular witch's magic?" I asked.

A sigh escaped the elder witch, "Yes and no. Their magic is... complicated. It's drawn from the world of death. They use magic like ours with wands but the other magic they summon is, well, blood."

"They use their own blood?" I asked in disbelief.

"Yes. They slice open their wrists and call forth their blood to summon the spirits from the other world, to summon their dark magic." She leaned over the table, "Now, it would be a lie if I said that you would never encounter a blood witch, but you will and you must be prepared." Her emerald eyes were serious and showed that she was indeed, wiser beyond her years.

"Have you encountered a blood witch?"

Pain and sadness wavered in her green gaze. Her brown brows knitted together causing her forehead to crease. She leaned back in her chair and glanced down at the floor. "I have. My mother. And I was the only one who could stop her." Her emerald eyes locked with mine. "I had to murder my own mother. Anyone you know could turn into a blood witch and that is why you must be prepared."

I knew the life of an Elder was nothing easy but I never knew it could be so... sad. The life of any witch was not always complete bliss. But what would my life be since I am the prophet? Will I be forced to kill someone I loved and held dear?

Elder Arya rose from her chair, "Now, I shall teach you defensive magic against blood magic." She retrieved her black wand from her cloak. "If a blood witch's magic is summoned forth and aimed at you this is the spell you would use to counter the attack." She closed her eyes and held her wand before her,

"Oh, light of the right come and bless on this night."

A pure white light flowed from the tip of her wand and split into tiny silver streaks of magic. They shimmered within the air and wrapped around Elder Arya forming some sort of protection barrier. She was encased in a holy light, the magic entwined around her and flowed like streams of water. Glittering wisps of magic fluttered through the air. She lashed her wand through the air and the magic surrounding her shot in silver streaks forward, seeking an opponent. Elder Arya called back the magic and it flowed back into the tip of her wand like smoky water. "If there was a blood witch before me then they would have been encased in my magic."

"And what happens when the magic surrounds them?"

Despair flickered in her emerald eyes, "They die. The pureness of the magic rips away the dark magic from their body, but that darkness has attached itself to their soul. Therefore, their soul is also ripped away from their body."

I peered down into my lap, my hands tightly gripping the handle of my wand. Could I really kill someone? Or will I be weak and allow them to live? My eyes stared upon the Elder that was seated before me. She found it in herself to kill her own mother, from the look in her eyes I knew it troubled her. That was something she would have to live with for the rest of her life.

"You must be prepared for anything." Elder Arya spoke quietly.

"And what if I'm not?"

Her emerald eyes locked with mine. "Then, you die."

* * *

Elder Arya's words stuck with me throughout the day, echoing in the back of my mind. During lunch I sat alone, mindlessly picking at my food and barely paying attention to the things happening around me. The caw of a raven rang in my ears as it landed on the wooden table before me. Its feathers were sleek and black. Its beady dark eyes stared upon me. Then a familiar, unwanted person approached the table behind the raven. Danielle smirked and seated herself in a chair across from me. Her fiery hair had been straightened and parted down the middle, the rest sweeping just a little past her shoulders. She propped her head on her hand and raised a finely plucked eyebrow at me.

"What do you want?"

She put on an act of seeming offended by my tone of voice. "Why, no hello? You just assume I want something?"

I leaned back in my chair. "I know that for some reason you don't like me. So I ask again, *what do you want*?" I crossed my arms over my chest.

Her face turned serious and she too leaned back in her chair, her eyes studying me. "I would like for you to join my coven."

"And why would you want me too?"

She leaned across the table, her breasts almost falling out of her white tank top. "Because, the goddess has marked you and given you strong magic." The last words she spoke whispered from her red masked lips. "And you have a connection into the veil."

"Why does any of that matter to you?" I raised a quizzical eyebrow to her.

"I have my reasons." She leaned back and crossed her arms over her chest.

"And you think that I would just agree to join you? Someone who has been rude to me since the moment I got here?"

She rose from her chair, planted her hands on the top of the table, leaned down, and stared into my eyes. "If you are smart, you would make a friend of me and not an enemy."

Matching her stern gaze I stood from my chair. "And if you had any brain in that head of yours you would know that threats do not scare me."

A smirk formed on her lips as her eyebrow raised. "This coming from someone that hasn't stood up to me before." She walked around the table and whispered into my ear, "Being the prophet child doesn't make you invincible."

With that, she walked away followed by her raven. As she approached the doors another person entered into the dining room. Their white hair was hard to miss. The two girls shared disgusted glances as they passed one another. Snow rolled her blue eyes and scuffed. Soon, the short girl stood before me. "Seeing the she-demon always downs my mood."

"Well, at least you didn't have the pleasure of sitting down and having a nice chat with her." I sighed and seated myself back in my chair.

"I could only imagine how wonderful that conversation must have been." She sat down at the table and leaned back in the chair. "What did the Queen B want?"

"She asked me to join her coven."

Snow's white eyebrows raised in curiosity and shock. "Sisters of the Night? Don't do it. It's nothing but trouble."

"What do they do? How many people are even in her coven?"

She sighed and bit her bottom lip. "Her and five others. They are pretty much the stuck up kids of the Elders. I like to call them the Prissy Clique."

"And what does this *Prissy Clique* do?" I asked again. It seemed as though she were avoiding my question.

"I honestly don't know, they are very secretive. But I was given the chance to join them and when I refused, well they weren't so happy about my answer."

"Did they do anything to you?"

She peered down at the table, the tip of her nail traced along the wooden details. "Mostly it was Danielle. She taunted and teased me. Then one day I grew tired of it and requested a duel between us. It was a close match, very close but Elder Arya stopped us before the match came to an end." Snow chuckled. "Apparently, magical matches aren't allowed on Council Hall grounds. And since then Danielle's constant harassment has slowed down, but only because I decided to stand up for myself."

"She told me being the prophet child didn't make me invincible. So now, I'm guessing I have to prepare myself for her torture?" A sigh escaped me as I rubbed my temples.

"Not if you stand up to her. She may act tough but I know some part of her fears you. She likes a challenge."

"But I don't want to fight. I came here to learn who I am and what I'm destined to do. I don't have time for petty girls."

Snow stood from the chair and kneeled before me, making herself eyelevel with me. "Don't you worry that pretty little head of yours. Snow has your back." Her bright blue eyes warmed with friendliness and a smile formed on her lips.

I smiled back to her, "Thank you."

* * *

Returning to my room I was greeted by Salem and Luna. I fed them bits of chicken from my lunch. They purred happily as they ate away at the chicken bits. As usual Nana was seated on the couch knitting away at the scarf. She smiled warmly as I seated myself beside her. "And what was today's lesson about, my dear?"

Taking off my sandals I kicked my feet up onto the coffee table, "Elder Arya told me about Blood Witches and taught me a spell to protect myself against them. If I were to ever encounter one that is."

The smile faded away from Nana's aged face as she stared upon me. A sigh escaped her as she set down her scarf. "Blood Witches are a disgrace to the witch community. They bring shame down upon us. Make us all look like evil beings from the underworld."

"Have you ever met a blood witch?" I propped my elbow on the back of the couch and rested my head upon my hand as I watched the older woman.

"As old as I am I have encountered many things in my lifetime. Blood witches unfortunately being one. I've had my share of duels against witches but when I found myself battling against one I quickly found myself fighting against something that was not from this world, but from the next."

"The dead." I whispered.

She slowly nodded her head. "Their magic is fueled by death, sorrow, grief, madness. Once a witch turns most of their sanity leaves them. They are no longer the witch they were before."

"Did a person you know convert?"

Pain flickered in her dark eyes. "My younger brother. We fought but my father was the one to end his life." Tears glistened in her eyes. I had never seen my Nana cry before. Never seen her feel pain. Reaching over, I grasped her aged hand.

"Life is not always easy. There are many obstacles and challenges within it. But the moment you were born I knew that someday you would be faced with many difficult things. I tried my best to give you happy memories, a wonderful childhood. But no matter how hard I tried an obstacle would arise."

"Nana, my childhood was filled with love. My life now is filled with love, thanks to you. I know life won't be easy for me but I'm preparing myself for the challenges that I will have to face someday."

A sad kind of smile spread across her lips. Her hand brushed some of my hair behind my ear. "You are growing into a strong young woman. Much like your mother." A hint of proudness flickered in her eyes. I knew I reminded her so much of her daughter, my mother. From looks, to personality, to creativeness. All these things Nana told me I inherited from the woman that gave birth to me but I couldn't help but wonder, what did I inherit from my father?

"Hey Nana, what else did I inherit from my dad besides my one eye color?"

Her eyes seemed to study me. Looking me up and down. "Your height definitely came from your father; your mother is a short woman. Much like myself." She chuckled. "You have his loving heart. He cared for every living thing. Your mother was a loving woman as well but your father's heart was more open and caring." Her eyes warmed with thoughts of my parents as she spoke about them. Her fingers brushed through my thick dark hair. "And your hair came from your father as well."

If I closed my eyes I could imagine them, my parents. My short mother next to my tall father. Their green and brown eyes staring lovingly into one another's. Happy smiles crossing their faces. I even imagined my mother holding a baby in her arms. Me. I wondered what it felt like to be held by them, loved by them. There was an emptiness in my heart, a void. I wanted so badly to meet the people who created me. Someday, I would. Deep within myself I knew that day would come. My hand reached up clasped around the silver locket that hung from my neck.

Nana's hand patted my lap, "That day is coming, Willow. I promise." She said to me as if she read my mind. She yawned and stood from the couch. "Now, it's time for this old woman to go to bed. Goodnight, my dear."

* * *

The following day, after my lesson with Elder Arya, Snow and I met up in the garden once again. We sat on the marble bench staring into the blue sky, not a cloud was in sight. The sun shone brightly, the heat of the day beating down on us. A slight breeze swept past us, causing Snow's long white hair to float along the wind. Our familiars walked along the edge of the fountain's last circular level, being careful not to fall into the water.

"Willow, you lived amongst the humans for most of your life, right?" Snow asked, holding her hand over her eyes shading them from the brightness of the sun.

"Well Nana and I lived in hiding really, we only went into the human towns if we needed certain foods, clothes, or cooking items." Playing around with my hair I braided a few strands together and scattered several more braids throughout my locks.

"What was it like? The humans? The towns?" Her blue eyes sparked with curiosity.

"Humans look like we do, the only difference being is that they don't use magic. The towns were different in each place we lived. Some were nothing extraordinary and others were massive and busy. People crowded the streets, hundreds of different shops to visit. The foods varied in different towns and cities." As I spoke I could imagine the smells of freshly baked foods, the smell of pastries filtering through the air. The sound of children's laughter. Suddenly, I found myself missing that.

"The human world sounds interesting."

"Have you never visited any cities or towns?"

"I've never left the council hall."

My mouth gaped open in surprise. "You mean, you've *never* left this place?"

She chuckled at my shock. "Nope. The children of witches never go into the human world, not until they are of age. Only adult witches can journey out."

"Let me guess, another law huh?"

She shrugged her shoulders, "Unfortunately."

"So, what age are you allowed to leave?"

"Twenty-one. The witches don't follow human age restrictions. They don't think that eighteen is an adult age, they say you are still a teenager. So, the age is twenty-one."

"Why not twenty?"

"Because, you have just transitioned from being a teenager

into an adult. They think you are still too naïve so they make you wait another year."

I shook my head, "Why so many weird rules and laws?"

"Everyone has their own set of rules they have to follow, no matter how stupid they sound."

I found myself staring at the girl that sat beside me. She had never left these grounds, never journeyed out and discovered what the world was like. Hidden away in the walls of that building. And now, I too was being locked away.

"They've finally lifted that eight o'clock curfew by the way." Snow said.

"Good, I missed coming out here at night." I broke my gaze away from the girl and watched my familiars snooze in the grass. "Why did they lift it?"

"Because no Exorcist will be foolish enough to attack a place where hundreds of witches live, along with gargoyles. Plus, it was just the one guy you saw anyways, he wouldn't be that stupid to do anything."

The sound of the gate creaking open sounded through the air. Snow and I peered over our shoulders to see a woman approaching us. A woman I knew to be wary of. Her white straight hair was bright in the sun's light. Her piercing blue eyes stared upon me as she came closer to the bench we were sitting on. Snow quickly stood from the bench. "Hello, mother."

The woman shot one more disgusted look my way before turning her attention to her daughter. "You are late for your daily lesson, come with me. *Now*."

"Yes, mother." Snow followed after the woman, Frost scurried up her legs and perched on her shoulder. Calling out she said, "See you at dinner, Willow!"

Elder Nehemiah peered back with anger and grabbed Snow's hand. Hurriedly, they left the garden. Salem and Luna leapt onto the bench were Snow sat. The two cats peered off where the women had disappeared. "Elder Nehemiah gives me the urge to claw her eyes out, especially after what she said to you." Luna said.

"Now, sister you know we cannot do that. Unfortunately." Salem said.

Reaching over I petted the cats on their heads. "Snow said that children and teenage witches weren't allowed in the human world."

"That is correct." Salem said.

"Then, since I'm here at the council hall now I won't be able to see my parents."

Luna and Salem eyed each other for a brief moment. "Unless they visit you here, Willow." Luna stated.

"Do they even know I'm here?"

Salem placed his paw over my hand. "Ask your grandmother. She might be able to contact your parents."

Standing from the bench I made my toward the gate and left the garden, my familiars following close behind me. I entered into the building and ascended up the stairs to my room. Opening the door, I called out for Nana. No one answered me. I knocked on her door and there was still no answer. I opened the door to find that she wasn't in her room. *Where could she be?*

Chapter Nine:
The Girl's Parents

"Elder Esmerelda, odd to see you're the only one in the council room." I said as I approached the stone table where the woman sat.

Her brown eyes took me in. "Us Elders are not always in this room. We have lives as well, Anora." She removed her glasses and placed them down. "Now, what brings you here?"

"I came here to talk about Willow's parents."

Esmerelda raised an eyebrow. "What of them?"

"She wishes to meet them. I would like to take her to visit them."

The Elder shook her head. "No. The child is not to leave these grounds again. It is against the rules for an underage witch to go into the human world."

"You forget that she spent most of her life in the human world." I said sternly.

"I forget nothing. The child never technically lived amongst the humans. You only took her into the towns when you needed something." She crossed her arms over her chest.

A sigh escaped me. "The girl needs to meet her parents."

"Does she really need too, now? Why can't she wait till she is an adult and is allowed to venture into the human world?"

I was growing impatient with the woman. "Elder

Esmerelda, I demand that you let the girl see her parents."

Anger flickered in her dark eyes. "*You demand?* You are in no position to be making demands, Anora." She stood from the table and stepped down from the upraised floor. Esmerelda stood before me, locking her dark eyes with mine.

"I was once on this council. I should be allowed to do this one single thing for my granddaughter."

"Exactly, you *were* an Elder but no longer. You've done many things for the girl that went against our rules and laws." Her tone of voice changed as she spoke. "You should be brought before the council and pay for the laws you broke."

My voice lowered and I took a step closer to the woman. "Under the circumstances I'm sure at least half of the Elders would vote in my favor. I have done many things for the witches, *good* things." I looked her deep in the eye. "Even for you, Sister Esmerelda."

She let out a sigh and rubbed her forehead. "Let's make a compromise. I'll contact her parents and have them visit her, here. Is that good enough for you?"

"Better than nothing I suppose. When can her parents come?"

"I have to contact them first and then make plans accordingly. I'll let you know when I find out anything. Alright?"

I felt defeated somewhat but this was the best I could do for Willow. For now. I nodded my head to the Elder and turned my back to the woman. As I approached the doors she called out to me. I stopped and peered over my shoulder at her. A smirk was formed on her lips as she drew forth her wand. "You forgot one thing, Anora. The greeting of Elders."

A chuckled escaped me, "You said so yourself that I am no longer an Elder."

Esmerelda waltzed toward me, slowly. Twirling her wand in her hands. "It is still tradition even for an ex Elder. Now present your wand, Anora."

I fully faced her with an eyebrow raised. I knew what she was doing. Proving herself. Doing as she asked I drew forth my wand from my pocket and presented it. A sphere of light ignited on the tip of it. Elder Esmerelda's doing the same. Together the spheres lifted from our wands and into the air. They danced around one another, twirling, spiraling. Then they collided. An explosion of magic flickered before our eyes. Wisps of magic fluttered down to the ground and dispersed. Looking at the Elder before me, her smile widened. "I'm still more powerful than you, Anora." She felt the need to remind me. As if I had forgotten.

"But we all know that Willow is stronger than me and even you, Esmerelda."

The smile faded away from her face. The corner of her lips dropping. The wrinkles around her eyes creased as she narrowed her brown eyes at me. Her nostrils snarled as her brows kitted together in annoyance. "Not yet she isn't."

"Ah yes, but one day she will be." I smiled at her and left the room.

Chapter Ten:
Shapeshifting

Today Elder Arya didn't fetch me for morning lessons, instead she told me to wait for her in the scholar room. Turning the knob on the door I entered into the candle lit room. I seated myself in a chair and waited for the Elder to come. Several minutes seemed to pass by with no sign of Arya anywhere. My eyes kept watch on the door as I impatiently waited. Soon, the door opened but Elder Arya was not who entered the room. Instead a massive wolf prowled toward me. Its' fur was a dark brown, its deep green eyes watched me. The creature seemed... intelligent, knowing. I stood from my chair and grasped my wand, holding it before me. The wolf stood before me, its eyes flickered to the wand in my hand. It nudged the tip of my wand with its nose. This creature did not fear me. It acted so differently than a wild animal. Like it knew who I was. As I peered into the creature's eyes realization struck at me.

"Elder Arya?"

The wolf nodded its head to me and soon its body began to glow. Glitters of silver magic began to manifest from its body. Fluttering down to the ground. Then it began to morph, the wolf's body turning human. Soon, Elder Arya stood before me. Her black robe draped over her body, her brown hair cascading down her back in curls. "And can you guess what today's lesson shall be about?"

"Shapeshifting." Excitement bubbled inside of me.

"Exactly. Shapeshifting is a special form of magic. It

enables you to transform into any creature of your choosing and stay in that form for as long as you wish."

"Are wolves your favorite animal?"

She chuckled, "Ah yes. Thought it would be fun to walk in here as a wolf."

"Elder Arya, what familiar do you have?"

"That should be obvious, Willow." She winked an emerald eye at me.

"A wolf, I'm guessing. How come I've never seen or met your familiar?"

She sighed, "She prefers to stay in the room. Now, I would like for you to shapeshift. Speak these words, *Oh body of mine morph into the creature of my choosing. The soul and body of a wolf I call forth.* Of course you can choose any animal you wish."

Drawing forth my black wood wand I repeated those words, *"Oh body of mine morph into the creature of my choosing. The soul and body of a cat I call forth."*

A tingling sensation spread across my body. The magic in my veins thrumming. I felt myself shrinking in height and weight. A tail sprouting from my skin. My legs and arms turning into furry black paws. Two ears popped up on my head and a meow escaped me. The transformation was painless. I stretched out my newly morphed limbs. My tail twitched behind me. My tongue ran across my feline fangs. I gazed up at the Elder that stood before me, she seemed like a giant.

"Strange, isn't it?" She giggled and kneeled down before me. Her fingers delicately stroked my head. "Good job, Savior."

Once again, she called me Savior. She believes that I can save the witches. But can I?

"Now, to transform into your human body I need you to focus. Concentrate on what it felt like to have fingers and toes. The way it felt to walk on two legs. The sound of your own voice."

Closing my eyes, I imagined my human body. I imagined

what it felt like to walk barefoot across plush grass. I remembered what it felt like to have a cool breeze sweep across my skin. The wind blowing through my dark hair. Suddenly, my feline body began to tingle. Glittering wisps of magic encased my body, swirling around me. My paws turned into hands and feet. My body grew in height and my fur disappeared and was replaced by pale skin. I found myself to be the same height as Elder Arya. A look of pride flickered in her eyes as a smile spread across her lips. "You know, it's not easy for every witch to shapeshift. It's tricky for some to return to their human form."

"Am I unlocking the other half of my magic?"

Her smile brightened. "Yes, Willow."

"I wonder what a witch in animal form would look like in the veil. Like, would the whole body glow with magic?"

"Good question, Willow. The only way to find out the answer is to see for yourself." Elder Arya grasped her wand, *"Oh body of mine morph into the creature of my choosing. The soul and body of a wolf I call forth."* Her body was encased in streams of magic and a wolf soon stood before me.

Closing my eyes, I focused on my connection to the veil. Opening my senses to it. I focused on the thrum of magic coursing through my veins. The burn and heat of it. I found my line of connection into the veil, my mind and soul grasped ahold of it. An explosion of light encased my mind and I had entered into the veil. Opening my eyes, I saw that everything was bright. I could sense the magic in the air around me, breathe it in. See the glittering, colorful wisps of it. I focused on the wolf before me. The body of the creature was a ghostly white, it glowed like a holy light. Its green eyes gleamed. Iridescent flickers of magic fluttered down from the wolf like a light rain fall. The magic poured from its being. A line of connection stretched out from the wolf's body and into the air above it. Suddenly the wisps falling from the wolf's body began to circle around it, spiraling like a tornado of magic. The Elder's human body was forming and soon Arya stood before me. Her body did not glow like the animal's did but I could still see the magic that coursed through her veins.

"What did you see?" She asked.

"The entire body of the wolf glowed."

"Then there is your answer. If you grow suspicious of an animal, you can enter into the veil to see if it is a witch in disguise." Clever, she was.

Closing off my senses to the veil the shimmering world around me faded away. "I'll remember that."

"Good. Today's lesson is over, I'll see you tomorrow." She nodded her head to me and left the room.

* * *

Entering into the dining hall my nostrils were assaulted with the smell of pancakes and maple syrup. My stomach growled with hunger as my mouth watered at the delicious scent. As I took my place in line I found Nana sitting alone at the beginning of one of the tables. Quickly making my plate I rushed over to her and seated myself across from her. Salem and Luna were eating away on strips of bacon.

"Good morning, Willow. What did you learn today?" Nana sipped on a steaming cup of coffee.

"Shapeshifting. I think that might be my favorite form of magic."

"Ah, that too is my favorite. I find it so interesting being able to shift into any creature of your choosing." A reminiscent look flickered in her gaze as she smiled.

"Hey Nana, why don't you have a familiar?" I had always been curious about this.

"Quick change of subject. But I had a familiar once, a falcon." She stared into her cup of coffee, her finger tracing along the rim of the glass. "My younger brother sacrificed my familiar to the dead. That was when we fought and that was when he died." Once again pain showed itself in her eyes.

"Why did you not find another familiar? I know it is impossible to replace the love you had for your other one, but still you could have found another."

She let out a sigh, "Because it is the duty of both the witch and the familiar to protect one another. I had failed on my part. Never again will I do that to another creature."

I glanced over at Salem and Luna. I would never forgive myself if anything were to happen to them. I understood how Nana felt. Nothing could replace my familiars, I loved them dearly. They were my friends, my family. I knew they felt the same for me.

"Excuse me, Willow. I have to leave and discuss a matter with the Elders." Nana stood from the table and left the dining hall, leaving Salem and Luna behind with me.

Stabbing my fork into the maple syrup soaked pancake I cut off a small piece and ate it. As I was chewing on my pancake a group of people entered the dining hall. Danielle was leading the girls behind her toward the table where I sat. Mentally sighing I prepared myself for whatever she was going to say. A snide smile spread across her cherry lips as she placed a hand on her hip. "I see your rodent friend isn't with you today."

"My friend's name is Snow and she isn't a rodent."

She shook her head as she chuckled. "Willow, I ask you one last time to join my coven."

"My answer is still no, Danielle."

Pulling out a chair she seated herself before me. The girls behind her stared right at me with expressionless faces. "Willow, joining us could be rewarding for you."

I raised an eyebrow to her, "Sounds like it would be more rewarding for *you* if I joined your coven. You have been persistent."

"I won't lie. You being the prophet and having a

connection to the veil is one of the reasons why."

Grabbing my plate I stood from the table, "My answer is no." I turned to leave but Danielle's group of girls stopped me from doing so. Each of them had their arms crossed over their chest with stern looks on their faces. I tried to move around them but they got in my way preventing me from leaving. Turning back to Danielle I saw a sly smirk on her face.

"I won't make it easy for you to reject my offer. You have something that is useful for me." She stood before me.

"You must not understand what the word no means." I raised one of my eyebrows to her.

She let out a chuckle. "Oh, I understand. But I don't take no for an answer."

"Hey! Why don't you go tend to your makeup, half your face smeared off." Snow pushed her way through the group of girls that stood in my way. A sigh of relief escaped me when the short girl came into sight.

"So now the little mouse decides to make an appearance." Danielle said.

Snow looped her arm through mine, "My friend and I are leaving. You and your pack of dogs should do the same." Together we pushed past Danielle's group of girls and left the dining hall.

Once we were alone in the hallway I let out a sigh. "Thanks for the save."

"Did they do anything to you?" Worry creased her face.

"No, but if you hadn't come along they might have."

"Let me guess, she asked you to join her coven again?"

"Yeah."

Snow shook her head, "She only asked me once. I don't know why she won't leave you alone."

"It's because I have a connection into the veil of magic. For someone reason that interests her." As I looked at Snow my eyes wondered down to her arm to find brown and green bruises blossoming on her skin. They looked like marks from fingers gripping her arm too hard. "Snow, what happened?"

She glanced down at her arm and moved her hand to cover the bruises. "It's nothing."

Frost popped his head out of her shirt pocket, "Do not lie to a friend, Snow."

The girl let out a sigh, "Really it's nothing. When my mother came to get me for my lesson the other day, when we were at the garden, she grabbed my arm too hard. Her anger just gets the best of her."

"Have you told the Elders about this?"

She let out a laugh, "My mother is an Elder. There's nothing they can say or do. Besides, it's nothing too serious. I'm fine, really." She forced a smile.

The sound of footsteps approached us, turning our attention down the hall we saw a boy seeming to be our age heading toward us. When he stood before us I noticed his height, he had to be at least six foot tall. His eyes were hazel and his black hair swooped down into those eyes of his. He wore a short sleeved shirt revealing his muscular arms.

"Hey Snow." He greeted her and then turned his attention to me, "I don't think I've met you before. My name is, Erin"

My eyes flickered over to Snow. She was staring at the guy like a puppy in love. "Hey, I'm Willow."

His gaze moved back over to Snow, "I'm getting some breakfast. Would you mind joining me? If you haven't eaten already." He shoved one of his hands in his pant pocket and the other combed through his shaggy dark hair.

"Yeah, sounds great." She smiled to him and together they walked into the dining hall.

"They would make a cute couple." I said.

"Indeed they would." Salem and Luna agreed as they brushed against my legs.

As we walked down the hallway another person came into

view. They turned the corner and nearly ran into me. It was Elder Esmerelda. She greeted me with a nod of her head, "Hello Willow. I was just on my way to find you."

"What for?"

"Follow me."

Glancing down at my familiars, I trailed after the Elder. She led me toward the council room. Pulling open the doors I found Nana standing in the center of the room, waiting for us. The Elder and Nana greeted one another and turned their attention to me.

"Your grandmother has news that she wishes to share with you." Esmerelda nodded her head to Nana.

Nana approached me and grasped my hands in hers. A wide smile spread across her thin lips. "Willow, my dear. Your parents are coming to visit you."

* * *

"Really? Are you excited?" Snow's blue eyes widened with shock.

"A mixture of nervous and excited, I suppose." Glancing down at my bed, I traced patterns in the blanket with my finger. When Nana told me my parents were coming I cried with happiness but now growing anxiety ate away at my being.

"When are they coming?" She cocked her head to the side as her eyes watched me.

"A few weeks or so. They have some traveling to do." A sigh escaped my lips.

Snow's white brows creased with concern. "What's wrong?"

"It's just that I worry. What will they think of me? How will they react to seeing me?" My eyes stared out the window. "How will I react seeing them?" My fingers found themselves around the locket that hung from my neck.

Turning to meet Snow's eyes I saw a smile written upon her face. Her fingers brushed my hair behind my ear. "I think that you worry too much."

A small smile formed on my lips. "Maybe so."

Snow glanced over at the clock upon my nightstand. A sigh escaped her. "It's time for my daily lesson. I'll see you tonight for dinner." With that Snow rushed from the room, leaving me alone.

Standing from my bed I seated myself at my desk and set to work finishing my painting of the witch's council hall. All the picture needed was a background. Dipping my brush into a dark brown, black paint, my hand guided the brush along the paper. Eerie trees began to take shape upon the painting. The dark trees were leafless. In my painting it was late winter. Winter was the season of death while spring was the season of rebirth. Though of the two, winter was my favorite. My mind was put at ease as the brush stroked across the paper. Art was my escape from the world.

Chapter Eleven:
Snow's Lesson

"You're late, again Snow." My mother was standing by the door waiting for me. Her fingers tapped her arms as her eyebrow raised. A disappointed look was on her face.

Shutting the door behind me I said, "I'm sorry. I was hanging out with Willow. I'm only a few minutes late."

"Those few minutes could have been used for learning." My mother shook her head. "You know what this means. You know the rules when you arrive late for lessons."

My hands trembled. My knuckles already hurt as I watched my mother retrieve a thick wooden ruler from her desk. She cracked it down upon the desk twice, waiting for me to lay my hands across it. Slowly, I approached the desk and lay my hands flat against the cool wood. Raising the ruler in the air it struck down across my knuckles. The wood cracked against my skin. Already my knuckles were bleeding from the first strike. I held back my whimper of pain and forced back my tears. Again she raised it into the air and struck me again. She would continue to do this until she felt satisfied with my punishment. A few more hits and she was done.

Staring down at my hands I saw that blood gushed from my knuckles. The skin had been broken open. My tears dripped down into my blood. It splattered across the desk top. Even the ruler my mother used had my blood stained on it. Grabbing a tissue, she wiped the ruler clean and returned it to the drawer. "One day, you'll learn Snow." My mother was disappointed with me. She always was. Nothing I did or could do pleased her.

"Now, prepare for your lesson for today."

"No." I whispered.

My mother stopped walking. She peered over her shoulder and her eyebrow raised. "Excuse me?"

Straightening my back I repeated, "No."

"Yes, you will prepare for your lesson. Do not defy your mother." Her voice rose with anger.

"I don't want to be an Elder like you!" I shouted out of frustration. My bleeding hands balled into fists by my sides.

"You have no choice, Snow. Prepare for your lesson, *now*." My mother was angered. Her voice was demanding. This wouldn't be my first time standing up to her. But every time I did, it ended in blood. "It seems as though you never learn." Instead of striking me with a ruler her hand struck my face. My cheek throbbed in pain where her hand slapped me. "Your lesson for today is to learn obedience."

*　*　*

When my mother was finally finished with her punishments, I rushed into the bathroom and locked myself inside. My cheeks burned with pain. My knuckles bled. Tears streamed down my face. Turning the faucet handle on the sink, I placed my hands underneath the cool water. My blood turned the clear water into red, filling the sink. Grabbing a gauze from a drawer I wrapped it around my knuckles. Staring into the mirror I peered into my own face. I looked so pathetic. I was stronger than this, or at least I liked to believe I was. Mother didn't realize that her beatings would only make me stronger someday. Soon I'll be able to withstand the pain and I won't cry anymore.

As I looked at my own reflection my stomach grew sickened. I looked too much like my mother. We shared the same white hair and the same bright blue eyes. Gazing at my hair, I had decided. Grabbing my white wooden wand from my back jean pocket, I began to cast a spell. *"Oh, hair of mine. Grow as blue as a sapphire. Never again return to your natural state until I command it."*

    Blue glittering wisps of magic filtered from the end of my wand. They floated into the air and spiraled around my head. The magic infused into my hair. Slowly, my hair faded into a new color. It started from my roots. My hair was turning blue. A dark hue of it but with highlights of turquoise. Down my hair transformed, every strand all the way to my ends. My fingers brushed through my new hair. I loved it. And I would love to see my mother's reaction. Leaving the bathroom, I strutted into the living room. My mother caught sight of me. Her mouth gaped open and her hand clutched her chest. "What have you done?!" She exclaimed.

    Flipping my hair over my shoulder I said, "Decided to change my hair. Like it?"

    "I most certainly do not! Change it back right now or I will!" She drew forth her wooden wand.

    "You can try."

    Anger blazed in her eyes. Pointing her wand at me she chanted, *"Oh, magic of mine transform this girl's blue hair to what it once was."* Her magic fluttered toward me and as it tried to infuse into my hair, it bounced off. Confusion crossed my mother's face. "I don't understand." Her brows creased.

    "I'm the only one who can change my hair color. Thanks to one of *your* lessons I made it a binding spell that could only be unbound by me."

    Crossing her arms over her chest she said, "Well played."

Chapter Twelve:
Willow's Parents Arrive

A month has come and gone since I was told about my parents plan to visit me. Today was the day they would arrive. Today I would finally meet my parents. Nervousness built up inside of me. I didn't know when they would arrive. Elder Esmerelda said sometime during the afternoon they would be here. It was twelve now. A sigh escaped me as I stood by the entrance doors. My eyes had been watching the doors all morning. Waiting to see my parents walk through them.

    A hand gripping my shoulder startled me. Whirling around I came face to face with Snow. Her blue hair was tied into a messy bun on the top of her head. Though it took some time for me to get used to it, I quite liked it. It suited her more than her natural color. "Lunch is starting, come on let's eat."

    Her hand grabbed mine and she led me away from the doors. "Can we wait a few more minutes?" My eyes glanced back at the doors.

    "No. I don't think your parents would want you starving yourself waiting for them. Besides, someone will tell you when they're here." With that, Snow drug me off into the dining hall.

    Once we entered into the dining hall, disaster struck. Danielle of course had to confront us with her usual snarky attitude. Today her focus was on me. She strutted across the hall swinging her hips. She wore a skirt that was so short it would be in her best interest to not bend over. Or maybe she wore it for that exact purpose? Her top was more on the conservative side. It was a black short sleeved shirt. Nothing much to it. Her prissy face was especially caked with makeup today, more so than usual. When she approached us she flipped her curly, fiery hair over her shoulder. "News today is that little orphan Willow is finally meeting her parents."

My heart ached at her harsh words. "Hey, Queen B, lay off." Snow stood in front of me.

"You know, blue is such a trampy color. Perfectly suited for you." Danielle retorted.

"I've heard that red is the new tramp. Which lays more true with you." Snow crossed her arms over her chest.

Danielle's smirk was wiped from her face. "How dare you."

Snow took a step closer to the girl. "Don't you ever say something like that to Willow ever again. Or you'll be dealing with me."

"Trust me little mouse, you aren't much to deal with." With that, Danielle flipped her hair over her shoulder again and strutted off.

"Somehow she's managed to hit lower than rock bottom." She turned her blue eyes upon me. Worry flickered in them. She placed her hand on my shoulder. "You okay?"

"Yeah." My voice whispered from my lips.

"Don't let that she-demon ruin your day. Cheer up! Your parents are visiting today."

She led me over to the carts of food. Grabbing a plate, I began to pile crisp lettuce upon it. I didn't feel like eating much, I was so nervous I feared that my stomach might get sick. Once our plates were made we seated ourselves at a table. Frost scurried from Snow's shirt pocket and along her arm. She placed a few crackers upon the table and Frost set to eating them. Salem and Luna slept by my feet underneath the table. I didn't eat much of my lunch. I was lost in thought. My fork pushed around my salad on the plate.

"Willow?" An older woman's voice sounded from behind me.

Turning around I saw Elder Esmerelda. "Yes?"

"Your parents have arrived."

My heart leapt at her words. Without waiting for my familiars or the Elder, I raced out of the dining hall. I bounded through the long hallway and came into the entry room. And there standing before the doors, were two people. A man and a woman. My mother and father. I was lost for words as I stared upon them. They looked just like they did in their pictures. My hand clasped around the silver locket that hung from my neck. Tears burned in my eyes. At first, I walked towards them. I feared that this was only dream and as soon as I reached out for them, they would disappear. I dashed across the long room. They opened out their arms for me. I crashed into their embrace. They were here. They were real. This was no dream. Their arms tightened around me. Sounds of joyful laughter echoed around us. We were finally together. Our little family was united. I peered into their faces. Tears stained their cheeks. The whites of their eyes were blood shot. My father's eyes were a brilliant green, much like one of my eye colors. My mother's eyes were a warm auburn, like my other eye. Her hair was light brown and curled down to the middle of her back. My father's hair was as midnight as mine. He had slicked it over to the side. My hands reached towards their faces. One hand rested upon my father's cheek and the other rested upon my mother's.

"You're really here…" I whispered.

My mother's hand rested over mine, "We are, sweetheart." Tears streamed from her eyes.

"And we aren't going anywhere." My father added.

"We love you, Willow. Very dearly." My mother said as she brought me into her embrace once more. I breathed in her scent. She smelled so lovely. Like freshly bloomed flowers in spring.

Someone cleared their throat behind us. Breaking free of my mother's embrace we turned around to face Elder Esmerelda, Nana was standing just beside her. My mother's eyes widened as she stared at her. Nana's eyes glistened as tears formed within them. "Mother…"

"My Lucinda…"

My mother ran into Nana's arms. Together the women cried as they held one another. "It's been so long." My mother said.

"Too long, my daughter."

"I've haven't heard from you in years. I thought the worst had happened to you." Glancing over her shoulder at me she said, "Both of you."

"I'm sorry, Lucinda. But to ensure Willow's safety, I had to stop writing letters."

My mother nodded her head. "I understand."

Elder Esmerelda stepped toward my Nana and Mother. "I hate to breakup this lovely reunion but there's a matter that must be discussed."

Nana turned a warning gaze upon Esmerelda. "And what would that matter be, exactly?"

"The girl's parents will not be allowed to stay here."

"And why not?"

"The only reason that Willow is staying here is because she is the prophet child. The only reason you remain here is because you were once an Elder."

Stepping closer to the woman Nana said, "Since I was once an Elder then my family should be able to stay here."

Elder Esmerelda shook her head. "That no longer applies to you."

"Why are you doing this? Willow needs her parents!" Nana shouted with anger. My mother grasped Nana's arm, holding her back.

"Mother it is alright. We can visit Willow."

Nana shook her head, "She needs to be with her parents. Not trapped here."

"Nana," I approached her. "I'm not trapped. I understand why I need to be here, I'm the prophet."

Elder Esmerelda stepped over to me and placed a hand upon my shoulder, "Anora, the child understands. Why can't you?"

Glaring at her I said, "That doesn't mean I don't want my parents to stay here. I would love for them too."

She removed her hand from my shoulder. "One day, you all will understand." I couldn't help but feel like that was a threat. "It is time for them to leave, your lesson for today will begin in a few minutes."

"But they just got here!" I cried out. My parents were being taken away from me and I had only just met them.

My mother grasped ahold of my hands. "My dear, we'll visit you again. This isn't goodbye."

"Then why does it feel like it is?" Tears brimmed in my eyes.

Her fingers gently wiped away my tears. "We love you, Willow. More than anything in this world. We'll visit you again soon enough."

Wrapping my arms around her I said, "I love you, mom."

***

Approaching the scholar room, I opened the door and stepped inside. The candles lit aflame as they floated about the room. But Elder Arya was nowhere in sight. I questioned why she wasn't here. We usually met here for lessons. Leaving the room, I traveled down the hallways searching for Elder Arya. Finally, I bumped into her, literally.

"I'm so sorry." I said as I stumbled backward.

She laughed, "It's okay, Willow." Then her eyebrows

creased together, "Aren't you supposed to be visiting with your parents?"

"They left a little bit ago, Elder Esmerelda said I had a lesson today."

Arya shook her head, "No. I canceled today's lesson so you could spend time with your parents."

"Then why would Elder Esmerelda say that?" Anger began to burn inside of me.

"I don't know, Willow. I will go speak with her." Saying that, Arya hurried down the hallway to find Esmerelda and confront her.

Anger flamed inside of me. I could feel the magic rampaging through my veins. Elder Esmerelda had lied. Why? I didn't know. I didn't understand. Why was she keeping me away from my parents? Suddenly it seemed like the walls around me were closing in. My breathing became panicked. My head felt like it was spinning. I leaned my back against the wall. Now, I was beginning to feel like I was trapped here.

Snow spotted me sitting on the floor and rushed over to my side. "Willow? What's wrong?"

Lifting my head from my hands I answered her, "We're trapped here."

Snow let out a sigh and leaned against the wall beside me. Her arm snaked across my shoulders. "Only till we're twenty-one."

I shook my head. "You may be able to leave then. There's no promise that I will be able too. I'm the prophet, they'll keep me here."

"I'm sorry, Willow." Sympathy sounded in her voice.

Chapter Thirteen:
Captives

Leaving the Council Hall, despair hung over our heads. So badly, we had wanted to see our daughter. We had longed for that moment for so long and it was just taken from us. Our brief moment of reunion was torn from us. It felt as though Willow had been ripped from our very arms. Our hearts ached. We knew we would see her again, hopefully soon. Glancing behind us, my eyes met with Elder Esmerelda's. She was keeping a close watch upon us from the window. Making sure we left the grounds. Climbing onto our broom sticks, we took flight into the afternoon sky.

  As we zoomed through the clouds a strange feeling crept along my spine. A feeling as though someone were following us. Watching our every move. I glanced over at my husband. Our eyes met and I knew he felt that strange feeling as well. Reaching into our pockets, we retrieved our wands and readied ourselves. Just ahead of us two Exorcists appeared before our eyes. Their hands glowed with that holy light. From the looks in their eyes, there were two ways this could end to them. We died or we were blessed.

  Our brooms hovered within the air. The Exorcists white robes swayed along the currents of the wind. Their hoods were pulled over their heads. Peering over my shoulder, two more Exorcists appeared. Flanking us. We were trapped and outnumbered. If it were only the two we would have stood a fighting chance. Before us, another Exorcist floated into the clouds. As they lowered their hood I realized, this was the leader. Fear was struck into the very core of my being. The older man smiled wickedly to us. His white hair was nothing but wisps attached to the sides of his head. Upon his balding cranium was a glowing tattooed cross. The man's ghostly eyes were creased with wrinkles. His hands were aged and veiny with glowing crosses tattooed on them as well.

He stretched out his arms in welcome. "Ah, the prophet child's parents. What an honor it is to meet you." The man's voice was chilling. He spoke formerly but there was an undertone to his voice. An undertone of maliciousness.

My husband and I glanced questionably to one another. How did he know we were Willow's parents? A chuckle sounded from the man. "You are asking yourselves how I know you are the prophet's parents. I know many things. Call it a gift from God." He winked a blue eye.

"What do you want from us?" I questioned him.

"First, I believe we should formerly acquaint ourselves. I am the leader of the Exorcists. The Priest."

Silently he waited for our replies but we remained silent. The Priest nodded his head. "No worries, I shall learn your names soon enough since you are to be my captives." Snapping his fingers he motioned to his followers.

"Why are you doing this?" I shouted angrily.

As a chain was whipped around my body and my arms were restrained, he answered me, "To lure the prophet child out of hiding of course."

Chapter Fourteen:
Lives in Danger

Elder Arya began her magic lesson earlier than usual today. She approached the window, unlatched it, and thrust it open. Refreshing air filtered into the scholar room. My lungs breathed it in. Joining me in the center of the room, Elder Arya withdrew her wand. "Now, do you know any elemental magic?"

"Wind. Nana never taught me the other elements."

Moving aside from the window she said, "Show me."

Aiming my black wand toward the window, I chanted, *"Oh wind of nature I summon you forth."* A strong current of wind breezed into the room. The velvet drapes drifted along the breeze. The air wrapped around my being. It felt cool.

Elder Arya's brunette hair was rustled. A smile spread across her lips. "Good, very good. You know, as you are calling upon the wind, you can picture how you control it. You may turn the air around you into a tornado."

Stepping toward the window she extended her wand outside. *"Oh wind of nature I summon you forth!"* The clouds within the sky began to swirl. The wind turned into fast paced currents. Slowly, a tornado began to form. It touched ground but it did not move. Arya glanced over at me with a smirk. She moved her wand to the right, the tornado followed. She moved it to the left, it followed once more. She flicked her wand upward, the tornado leapt. I was in awe. There was so much I had to learn about magic.

Calling back her magic, the tornado dispersed. "Now, for the element of water, here's the words you must speak. *Oh, purest form of nature. Water, I summon you forth.*"

Peering out of the window, my eyes landed upon the fountain hidden within the garden. Pointing my wand in that direction I chanted, *"Oh, purest form of nature. Water, I summon you forth."*

The water did as it was commanded and slowly rose from the fountain. It swirled about within the air as it drifted along the currents of the wind, making its way to the window. The stream of water floated before me. Ripples rushed through it like tiny waves. The sun's light glistened upon the water's clear surface. Glancing over at Elder Arya, she nodded her approval. I sent the water back to where it belonged and turned to face the Elder beside me.

"Magic confuses me."

She cocked her head to the side, "How so?"

"For example, when you summon the dishes to wash themselves you don't always have to say the same incantation. But with shapeshifting and elemental magic, you do."

"Well, you cannot just say, *water I call you forth.* No. You have to speak to it's very essence. It's one element of life. You must speak clearly to it, to call it forth. With dishes, it's simple magic. You don't need to say much for them to wash themselves. As for shapeshifting, you need to be precise with your wording in order to transform into the animal you desire. Understand now?"

I nodded my head to her. "Yeah."

Suddenly, Nana burst through the door of the scholar room. A panicked look crossed her face. Rushing over to me, she grabbed my hands. "Nana, what's wrong?"

Glancing over at Elder Arya she said, "We need to go to the council room. *Now.*"

Rushing through the hallways, Nana held tightly onto my hand. Both Elder Arya and I were confused. Once we approached the council room doors, Nana thrust them open and dragged me into the room. The Elders were seated at their high table. They too seemed panicked and troubled. None of them bothered doing the greeting of the Elders. Something was terribly wrong. Elder Artemis rose from his chair and bowed a greeting our way.

"Hello again, Prophet Child." He spoke to me.

"Hello, Elder Artemis."

Enya spoke up, "Enough of the greetings. Tell the child what has happened." It has been awhile since I've last seen her and still her exotic beauty fascinated me.

Glancing back over to Elder Artemis I asked, "What's happened?"

"Your parents have been captured by the Exorcists." He said gravely.

My heart felt like it stopped beating for a moment. My stomach sank. "What?"

"A gargoyle scout said it saw your parents being taken away by five Exorcists." Artemis said.

"Then let's go rescue them!"

Each of the Elders glanced at one another, silent murmurs whispered from their lips. Elder Darrio was the one to speak up, "We cannot risk the lives of us to save two witches."

"They're my parents!" Tears burned within my eyes. My fists shook by my sides.

Elder Artemis spoke once more, "We will figure out a way to save them." He cut a sideward glance at Elder Darrio. "But we cannot do anything at this moment."

"Let me go. The only reason why they could have taken my parents is because I'm the prophet."

Elder Darrio shook his head. "You are truly foolish, still a child at mind. If you go to them, they will sever your link to the veil thus severing all of our links. Our magic will be lost. Do you not see what is at stake here?"

I hated to admit it, but Elder Darrio was right. I couldn't go to the Exorcists. Suddenly a plan formed within my mind. Perhaps I could go, but not alone of course. "What if I went with a group of witches? That way I wouldn't be alone and would have protection."

Elder Artemis seemed to think about this idea. His golden brows creased together as he thought. "It would be an ideal plan but as Elder Darrio has stated, we cannot risk your life or the connection to the veil." A sigh escaped him, "It is a no. We will form a plan to retrieve your parents, without putting you in danger."

"So now, you expect me to go about my day as if nothing has happened?" I asked bitterly.

Snow's mother, Elder Nehemiah spoke up, "Yes, that is exactly what we expect from you. Prophet child." She practically spat those last words out with disgust.

Elder Artemis spoke up, "We need for you to continue your training. At some point you will have to face the Exorcists if we are to stop them, but not now. It is too soon for you to be fighting. There is much you need to learn."

A defeated sigh escaped my lips. They were right. I wasn't strong enough to rescue my parents. Not now. Rushing out of the council room, I bounded down the hallways, and ran out the front doors. Dashing through the courtyard I came upon the entrance gate of the garden. Unlatching it, I walked inside. Walking down the stone pathway, I found myself standing before the fountain. Approaching a marble bench, I seated myself upon it. I needed fresh air. I needed to be alone and sort through my thoughts. My head rested in the palms of my hands. Tears streamed down my cheeks. I had only just saw my parents and now they had been stolen. Taken captive by our enemy. I felt so helpless, so powerless.

Goosebumps arose along my arms. I wasn't alone here, not anymore. Lifting my head from my hands, I peered around me. The garden seemed empty. It seemed as though I were the only soul here. But I knew that was not true. Retrieving my wand from the inside of my black knee high boot, I stood from the bench. My wand was held out before me. Once more, I felt like something was drawing me to the fence toward the back of the garden. I approached it hesitantly. But when I gazed out across the field I saw no one. Suddenly, a twig snapped above my head. Glancing upward, my eyes met with auburn.

The eyes of the exorcist boy. Leaping down from the tree, he stood before me. I never noticed his height before, he towered over me. Taking a step back, I aimed my wand at him. "Where are my parents?"

His eyes watched me closely. "They are with the Priest. At our home, the church." His voice was deep.

"Why are you here?" I questioned him.

"If you come to our home, then your parents will be set free."

"But then they'll sever my link to the veil."

He nodded his head. "It is a trap. There's no real winning in this situation for you."

"Why are you here!" My voice rose in frustration.

He cocked his head to the side, "I wish I could give you an answer. I don't know myself why I am here." He took a step toward me. "Perhaps it's because I find you fascinating. Or perhaps it's because I'm evil and want to do you harm, since you are the prophet."

"If you wished to do me harm, you would have done so by now."

A smirk crossed his thin lips. "You have a point, prophet child."

In our other times of meeting, he has not spoken quite as much as he is now. I found it odd. "You're just trying to mess with my head."

Those auburn eyes of his seemed to stare right into my soul. "Or perhaps I truly do find you interesting."

"How so?" I never lowered my wand.

"I appreciate an artistic mind."

"How did…"

He interrupted my question, "When I knocked you down in the town, paints spilled from your bag. You are an artist. A painter."

I shook my head. I couldn't allow him to get into my head. "Leave. Now."

Leaping over the fence he said, "We will meet again, Willow." Then, the Exorcist boy disappeared in the light of day.

A few moments had passed and the sound of hurried footsteps rushed toward me. Peering over my shoulder, I saw long blue hair traveling across the wind like ocean waves. Snow stood before me. Her brows were creased with worry, sadness, and pity. Without saying a word, she tossed her arms around me and embraced me. She has heard the news about my parents capture. My head rested upon her shoulder. In this moment I wanted to cry but no tears could be found. All I felt was empty. Powerless. What was the point of being the prophet and having such "strong" magic, if I couldn't use it to save the people I loved?

Chapter Fifteen: Prisoners

Together my husband and I were locked inside a cell. Our wrists and ankles chained, shackles rattled across the floor if we moved. The Exorcists made sure we were separated. My husband was across the long cell, chained to the wall. And here I sat, several feet away from him chained like an animal. We had yet to be blessed, thankfully we still had our magic. But no longer did we possess our wands. They were confiscated from us the moment we were captured. Where did they put them and our brooms? I had no clue. As I sat here my mind began to form plans of escape but the two of us stood no chance here. We were in the Exorcist home, hundreds of them lived here in this "church". We would die before we ever stepped foot out of this place.

As a sigh escaped my lips I leaned my head back against the wall. My eyes gazed upon the paintings above me. The ceiling was decorated in many painted pictures. They depicted Exorcists kneeling to the ground before their "God". The man stood tall above them with his arms stretched out wide. A holy light surrounded his being. These people's God was depicted differently than that of the human's God. The man had a cleanly shaven head with a glowing tattoo of a cross etched into his scalp. Within the palms of his hands were crosses as well. Beams of light emanated from them. That was what they used to "bless" us witches.

They believed us to be touched by the devil's hand. That our souls were tainted. Our beliefs and magic were thought to be wrong since we did not bow before their "God". They prayed to him, asking him to grant them with powers to rid us of our "evil". And he answered their prayers. He gifted to them the power to destroy our link to our veil of magic.

It was strangely odd how a God would gift people with powers to destroy. It was odd how a *God* would gift simple humans this. Much of this did not make sense to me. Though, I knew little about the Exorcists past. All I knew was that they were set on destroying us and the few stories I've heard of.

My daughter was marked as the Prophet child. Marked as the one to end this war between the witches and Exorcists. Our goddess answered our sorrow and cries when she witnessed the terror the Exorcists were putting on our kind. Blessing and killing mothers, fathers, and children. Slaughtering our familiars. The tales of the first war were truly horrific. So many deaths and loses. So much sorrow. Only did our people pray to our goddess when we felt truly defeated. In the story of the first war, it was said that the goddess emerged from the veil of magic and spoke to the witches. She told them of a prophecy, that a Prophet child shall be born five hundred years later. The child would be marked with the goddess's symbol, the triple moons. The child would be gifted with strong magic. Part of the goddess's sacred powers. The Prophet would be able to bring an end to our enemy. But no one understood why the child couldn't be born then and save them. When the witches questioned the goddess, she did not answer them.

I shook my head. Our past wars have carried on throughout the years. The witches were forced to go into hiding out of fear. What was the goddess's purpose in waiting five hundred years? Was this some sort of lesson? Or something we would never come to understand?

Candle light flickered down the hallway and approached the

cell we were held in. As it came closer, I saw that it was the Priest. A wicked smile formed on his lips. He thinks he has won. "Your daughter should be on her way here to save you two."

I shook my head, "The council won't allow her to leave."

A chuckle escaped him. "Oh, you think she'll listen to the council when she thinks her parents are in danger?"

I bit my lip. I hoped she would listen. I hoped she would stay away. He saw my fear and my doubts. The Priest stretched out his right hand. The cross tattooed upon his palm glowed. My eyes traced along the glowing intricate lines that made up the cross. It appeared as though some words were also tattooed within the shape of it. But they were small and hard to read. I could only guess they were scriptures from their "bible". His hand slipped in between the spaces of the bars, his palm facing me. A cold sweat swept over my body. It beaded down my brow as I stared upon the glowing cross. Fear trailed its cold fingers along my spine causing my being to shudder. The Priest laughed at this, mocking my fear. Pulling his hand back, he began to walk down the hallway.

"Willow will be here soon enough." His voice echoed down the hall.

Chapter Sixteen:
Friends and a Plan

The rain steadily poured. The sky was gray with misery. Thunder roared angrily overhead. Rain droplets raced down my window. My head was leaned against the cool glass. My eyes watched as the sky lit up with streaks of white lightning. The weather matched my mood perfectly. As of now, I was drowning in my own self-pity.

Outside my bedroom door sounded the meows of Salem and Luna. I had wanted to be alone so I locked myself within my room. Nana has come and knocked a few times trying to persuade me to come out. But I never left. I knew she set a tray of food for me in front of the door but I simply wasn't hungry. I was too upset to eat.

All that was on my mind was my parents. Being held captive by the Exorcists. I could only imagine what was happening to them, I feared the worst. Was their magic already taken from them? Were they even still alive? My stomach grew sickened as I thought this.

Knock. Knock.

I didn't bother asking who's there. I didn't want to talk or see anyone. Wrapping my arms around my knees, I pulled them close to my chest, and rested my head upon them. I heard Snow's voice. She was casting magic trying to open my door. The door wouldn't budge. It was sealed with my magic.

A distressed sigh sounded from Snow. "Willow, please open the door. You've locked yourself away for almost a week now." I heard her picking up the tray of food by the door. "At least eat the food your Nana left for you."

My stomach growled, I was hungry. But I couldn't force myself to eat. A loud *boom* sounded outside the window as the sky lit up with lightning. The rain pelted down heavily. Salem and Luna meowed loudly. I knew they hated storms. A sigh escaped my lips as I approached the door and released my magic from it. Opening it, I was greeted with Snow's face. Her blue hair was pulled back into a long braid. Within her hands she held the tray of food. Salem and Luna brushed against my legs purring and then scurried off into my room.

"Can I come in?"

Stepping aside I allowed her into my room and shut the door behind her. She set down the tray of food on my desk and sat on the chair. Her round blue eyes stared out into the storm. She sighed and glanced over at me. "I'm sorry about your parents, Willow." She shook her head. "I'm not much comfort when it comes to this sort of thing. I don't know what to say except that I'm sorry."

Seating myself upon the bed, Luna crawled into my lap and silently purred. "Thank you, Snow." In truth, I'm glad she's here. Though I didn't wish to talk to anyone, I knew that at least Snow could boost my mood.

Moving from the chair, she sat on my bed before me. "So, what's the plan?"

I looked at her confused, "Plan?"

"To save your parents, silly."

A sigh escaped me, "There is no plan, Snow. The council forbids me to leave."

Leaning toward me she said, "The council won't have to

know."

I raised a brow to her, "They'll know when my parents are free."

"Then if they're free, the plan worked and no one was harmed."

"Snow, saving them won't be easy. They're being held captive by the Exorcists."

She shrugged her shoulders, "I know it won't be easy. That's why I'm going with you." She winked.

I shook my head. "No. It's too dangerous."

Salem and Luna spoke up. "We'll come along too."

"No. I'm not putting any of you in danger."

"We are your familiars. It is our job to protect you." Luna said.

"Even so, the four of us don't stand a chance against the Exorcists."

"That's why I've asked Erin to come along with us."

Before I could say anything to Snow, Nana entered the room. "And I'm coming as well."

"Nana…"

"My daughter, your mother, is in danger. I will do anything to get her back. Your father as well."

A knocking sounded at the door of our room. Nana left to see who it was. When she returned, Erin was with her. Peering over at Snow I saw that same puppy in love look on her face.

Standing at the door, he stood there sheepishly. His hand brushed through his hair. "Sorry I'm late."

"It's okay. We haven't made any plans yet." Snow said to him.

Erin's hazel eyes glanced around the room, "So it's only us four?"

Salem and Luna answered him, "Six." They said in unison.

Frost finally made his appearance, peeping his head out of Snow's shirt pocket. "Seven."

Erin nodded his head. "Then I guess my familiar can tag along as well. That would make eight."

Standing from the bed I said, "You guys don't have to do this. It's too dangerous."

Nana approached me and rested her hand on my shoulder. "We want to do this. Each of us knows the risks. But we are willing to do this."

My eyes met with Erin's. "Then why are you doing this? You barely know me."

He glanced over at Snow and back to me. "I've lost both of my parents. And I don't want the same happening to you."

"Thank you, Erin."

He gave me a shy smile and nodded his head to me.

"So, what exactly is the plan?" I asked.

Snow glanced over at Nana. "The council does have a point, as much as I hate to admit it. There's still much you must learn about magic. Allow Elder Arya to give you a few more lessons and then we shall make a plan." Nana said.

I nodded my head. They were right. If I wanted to stand a chance against the Exorcists, I needed to learn more magic. "Alright."

Snow approached me and placed a hand on my shoulder. "Don't worry, we'll get your parents back and kick some Exorcist ass."

Chapter Seventeen:
Continuing Our Lesson

The following morning, I met with Elder Arya in the scholar room to continue my magic lesson that was disturbed due to my parent's capture. The candles danced about within the air, flames already burning upon their wicks. Elder Arya was leaned against the wall, her mossy green eyes staring into the clear sky of the day.

As the door clicked shut behind me, her gaze found mine. A smile spread across her lips. "Good morning, Willow. Are you ready to continue our lesson over the elements?"

"Yes."

Elder Arya drew forth her wand from her black cloak, "We already covered wind and water, correct?" I nodded my head. "Then there's fire and earth."

Stepping away from the window, she reached up and grabbed a candle from the air. Extending her arm, she pointed her wand toward the flame, *"Oh, fiery form of nature, I summon you forth!"*

The tiny flame danced about as the size of it began to increase. Slowly, it lifted from the wick and a fiery sphere formed within the air. Wisps of flames danced about. The sound of it crackled within my ears. Heat radiated from the sphere, the room growing increasingly hot. Sweat began to form upon my brow. Elder Arya's green eyes flickered over to me and the sphere began to shrink. It floated about within the air above the candle and drifted back down to the wick, returning itself to where it belonged. The tiny flame continued to burn upon the candle as she released her hold on it and it floated within the air.

"Now, you try it." She spoke.

My eyes glanced around the room upon all the floating candles. Grabbing one that was closet it to me, I stretched my arm out. Staring into the flame reminded me of the anger that burned deep within me. Frustration. Fear. Aiming the tip of wand toward the flame, I repeated, *"Oh, fiery form of nature, I summon you forth!"*

The small flame burst. Embers flew into the air. The fire engulfed the candle entirely. A yelp sounded from me as I released my hold on the candle. The flaming candle danced about within the air. Getting dangerously close to the crimson drapes.

"Willow, calm your magic. Call it back." Elder Arya instructed.

Aiming my wand toward the candle, I tried to extinguish the flame. But it did not obey my command. The flame intensified. Elder Arya grabbed my wrist and pointed my hand toward the window. The flaming candle flew across the room and into the sunny sky.

Arya's green eyes swam in concern. "Your emotions were connected to your magic, Willow. That was why it grew out of control and did not obey. You must learn to disconnect your feelings from your magic."

Shamefully, I broke my gaze away from hers. I had fueled that fire with my own angry emotions. From the fire that burned deep within me. "I'm sorry. It won't happen again." I muttered.

Her hand softly gripped my shoulder. Peering into her eyes, I could see understanding. "I know you are upset about your parents, Willow." She shook her head, "My parents are gone from this world, Goddess watch over them." Tears brimmed within her eyes. "I am sorry this has happened, Willow. But the council is trying their best to form a plan to save your parents."

When Elder Arya glanced at me again, her brows creased with confusion. Her hand reached toward my face and her fingers brushed away my bangs. A gasp sounded from her lips. "Your mark..."

My fingers rubbed against my forehead where my mark would be. Nothing felt strange. "What happened?"

"There's more details to it now. You must have unlocked another portion of your power when your emotions fueled that magic."

Glancing around the room, I searched for a mirror but found none.

"Once our lesson is done for today, you may return to your room and examine your mark there." Elder Arya spoke. Walking toward the door, her hand gripped the knob. "Now, for the rest of your lesson, we will be outside."

So I won't burn down the council hall?

* * *

The cooling air danced along my skin. My floor length, lacey black skirt drifted along the breeze. My hair was brushed away from my face by the gentle wind. I hadn't realized it till now, that weeks, months, had passed since my arrival here. Time has passed me. So much has happened since the first day I arrived here. My life was turned upside down the day of my birthday. The day I learned I was the "prophet". Gazing into the clear sky, I wished for my old life. The days my Nana and I spent in that cottage home. The days I would spend painting under that old willow tree. I missed those simple days.

Elder Arya walked ahead and I followed close behind her. She led me toward the garden. The gate door creaked open as she gently pushed it. Walking along the path, we soon stood before the fountain.

Elder Arya stood there silently. Her black robe draped along her body and pooled by her ankles upon the stone path. The hood was lowered from her head, her brunette, curly locks cascaded down her back. Those emerald eyes of hers gazed into the glistening water in the fountain's lower ring. "I know things have been hard for you recently. I had hoped your lesson today would distract you. But I see you are still bothered. So, tomorrow and the day after you are free to do whatever you wish during those days. No lessons."

"Thank you." I said. A few free days would hopefully ease my mind and I could relax.

She smiled, "Now, let us finish this last thing and you are free to go." Stepping away from the fountain, she strayed from the stone path and walked along the grassy earth. Kneeling down to the ground, she drew forth her wand. "Now, just like the other forms of nature, you picture in your mind how you want the magic to shape the earth." Aiming her wand toward the ground, she spoke, *"Oh, earth beneath us, this form of nature, I summon forth!"*

Kneeling beside her, I watched as the ground stirred. A sprout blossomed from the dirt. Slowly leaves began to grow from the stem. A bud formed. Crimson petals began to bloom, fanning out. Delicately, Elder Arya's slim fingers brushed against the edges of the flower's petals.

Her emerald eyes glanced toward me, "Now, you try."

Nervously, I gripped my wand. Closing my eyes, I detached my feelings from my magic. Calming myself. Easing my fears and worries. Letting out a breath, I glanced down at the ground. Picturing a flower within my mind, I repeated, *"Oh, earth beneath us, this form of nature, I summon forth!"*

A flower began to blossom from the dirt. A beautiful lily began to grow. Its white petals then faded to pink toward the center. Tiny red dots sprinkled across the petals.

Elder Arya smiled at the flower. "You know," she spoke softly, "since I was a child, I've always wanted a daughter and her name would be Lily." There was a hint of sadness in her voice, her eyes. "But being a council member, makes it difficult to find love."

"Are there no men here you're interested in?" The question felt too personal to ask.

A light blush spread across her cheeks. "There is one man. Elder Artemis."

Part of me was relieved it wasn't Elder Darrio she was interested in. Elder Artemis seemed like a good man. When the other Elders were against me, he was on my side. "He seems like a good man."

Her smile widened. "He is."

Seeing her and Snow speaking of men that they adored, made me suddenly feel lonely. Gazing upon the lily, I began to wonder, when would I find the one for me?

Chapter Eighteen: Free Days

Early morning light filtered into my room through my opened curtains, bathing everything in a warm glow. The sun's light shone in my eyes awakening me from my land of dreams. Birds chirped outside the window, greeting the new day. Salem and Luna slept near my feet, silently purring. Their tails flickered. For a moment, I laid there, staring at the ceiling. Today, I could rest, give my mind a break. My plan was to sleep in this morning, but of course that didn't happen. I awoke the same time I did every day for morning lessons with Elder Arya.

Carefully, I got out of bed. Being sure not to disturb the sleeping cats. My feet quietly sounded against the black marble floor as I entered into the small living room. Nana was nowhere to be found, perhaps she was still asleep within her own bed.

My stomach growled. Peering at the clock upon the wall, I knew breakfast was being served down stairs. A groan sounded from me as I thought of Danielle. There was a chance I could bump into the ice queen today and that would throw my relaxing day right out the window. Another growl sounded from my stomach. Letting out a groan, I quietly walked back into my room to change.

Salem and Luna still slept upon the bed, curled next to each other. Smiling at them, I turned to face my closet. Opening the door, I began searching through my clothes. My fingers brushed against the lacey fabrics of long skirts and kimono cardigans. Grabbing a high waisted, long skirt, a black, short sleeved crop top, and a floral printed kimono, I began to dress myself. Tossing my pajamas in the hamper. Before I left my room, I peered at the mirror attached to the back of my door. Thin lines of black laced across my cheeks bones. Spirals danced along them, delicately. Sweeping aside my bangs, more lines danced across my skin. Above my brows the spirals danced together. No markings appeared between my brows. Stopping at the beginning of them. Covering my mark, I laced up my roman saddles, grabbed my wand and put it in the inside pocket of my kimono cardigan, and left the room.

    Walking down the stairs, my fingers glided across the railing. The halls were empty, which was odd. Venturing toward the dining room and pushing open the doors, I found there were very few souls to be found in here. There were people scattered around within the room. Sitting quietly eating their breakfast. I made my way over to the food carts and began to make a plate. So far, the ice queen hasn't shown herself. Quickly, I piled food on the plate. Pancakes, bacon, biscuits, and eggs.

    Once I had poured a glance of orange juice, I turned around to leave but my eyes met with Danielle's. A smirk formed upon her cherry red lips.

    Her hips swayed as she closed the distance between us. Flipping her curly, red hair over her shoulder, she spoke. "Hello, Willow. I see your rodent friend isn't with you today." I tried to step around her but she blocked me. "Join the Sisters of the Night."

    A sigh escaped me, "My answer is still no. Leave me alone, Danielle."

    Her eyes locked with mine. "If you change your mind, we'll be meeting tonight in the garden at midnight. I *hope* you'll be there." She leaned down and whispered in my ear, "I'd hate to see what would happen to the savior if she didn't show up."

Meeting her gaze, I said, "You wouldn't dare hurt me." My words were like a challenge. Tempting her. Teasing her. She wouldn't lay a hand on me, I was the prophet and the council wouldn't let it slide.

A chuckle sounded from her, "Oh, don't think that, Willow. There are many things I would dare do." Turning on her heel, she left the dining room, "Midnight, don't forget or I'll come looking for you." She called over her shoulder.

As Snow walked into the room, they glared at one another as they passed through the doors. Snow rolled her blue eyes and made her way over to the food carts where I still stood. She smiled to me and grabbed a plate. "What did the Queen B say to you?" She made her way down the carts piling food onto her plate.

Glancing back at the door, half expecting to see Danielle standing there, I said, "She asked me to join her little coven or whatever again."

Snow let out a groan and tilted her head back, "What does she not understand by the word *no*?"

"She told me their having a meeting tonight at midnight. She's expecting me to be there, basically threatened me if I don't show."

Snow's eyes met with mine as she raised a brow. "Are you going?"

Raising my brow in return, I said, "What do you think?"

Her lips pulled into a smirk, "I'll take that as a no." She poured herself a glass of milk. "If she threatened you, I wouldn't worry too much about it. She can't do much with you being the prophet plus I'd gladly teach her a lesson." She winked an eye.

Letting out a laugh, I said, "We both could teach her a thing or two."

Snow gestured toward a table, "Want to join me for breakfast or were you heading up stairs?"

Glancing back at the doors, I faced her again, "I can join

you."

Sliding into the chairs we set our plates down upon the table. No one was near us. Some of the people had already finished their breakfasts and left the dining hall. Others were scattered around the many tables eating alone.

"So, no morning lessons today?" Snow asked.

Taking a sip of orange juice, I answered her, "No, I'm free today and tomorrow. She wanted me to ease my mind since so much has happened lately."

"I would spend more time with you but my mom is strict with her lessons but I'll come by when I'm done." She smiled.

"I would like that." Glancing around us, I asked, "Where is everyone?"

Her eyes widened, "Oh! Everyone is preparing for Samhain! I told you it's our biggest celebration."

"But it's months from now. Isn't a little early to prepare?"

Snow leaned an elbow on the table, "Willow. It's our *biggest* celebration. We need to prepare early so we'll be ready for the celebration."

"What is the celebration?"

Snow took in a breath and closed her eyes. As if she were imagining it. "It's a beautiful masquerade. Dancing, music, and *plenty* of food. Dresses, tuxedos, and masks, which everyone wears. The elders do their greetings but sparks of colorful magic explode in the air and glitter down upon us. They do this at the beginning of the celebration and toward the end."

I could imagine the beautiful dresses. I could almost hear the music. A scene of people dancing around a large room wrapped around my mind. I could see the glitters of magic gently fluttering down and landing upon a crowd of masked people. "Why does everyone wear masks?" I questioned.

"It's an old tradition. Back in the old days, the witches wore them to confuse the spirits that crossed back over into our world when the veils were thin."

"The veil between the living and the dead." I said.

Snow nodded her head, "Exactly."

"Then I suppose blood witches enjoy that holiday as well. Since they seem to love the dead."

Snow stiffened for a moment. "It's also a night that we must be careful, those *witches* love to summon upon the spirits and make sacrifices right before them. They think it gives them more power." There was a distant look within her blue eyes. "From what I've been told about blood witches, I never want to meet one."

Stabbing at the eggs on my plate with my fork, I said, "Yeah, me too." But I had a feeling I would meet one someday.

The sound of heels echoed around the dining room. Peering over my shoulder, I watched a woman storm toward our table. Her blue eyes were locked on Snow. Her white hair bounced with every, heavy step she took. Snow let out a sigh as her mother approached the table. The woman crossed her arms over her chest and raised a thin brow to her daughter.

"Your morning lesson began a few minutes ago. You're late, *again*." She hissed the word.

Glancing toward Snow, I saw that her hand tightly gripped the fork she held. Her knuckles turned white. "I was having breakfast with, Willow."

Elder Nehemiah glared at me. Her lip curled into disgust. Scowling at her daughter once more, she said, "Return to the room, *immediately*."

Giving me one, last glare, she turned on her heel and stormed from the dining room. Echoes sounded through the hall as she walked away.

Snow let out a groan. "Sorry, Willow. I'll come to your room later after my lessons." She gave me a weary smile before standing from the table and following after her mother.

I wanted to reach out and grab her hand. I wasn't oblivious. I knew her mother hit her. But there was nothing I could do.

Snow refused to talk to me about it and she refused to go to the council. But, what if I went to them? Could they help her? Or would they ignore the problem since Nehemiah was an Elder?

Glancing toward the door, I watched as my friend left and I knew that her mother wasn't going to be kind when they got to their room. It wasn't my place to interfere, to stick my nose in their business. I was torn. What should I do?

Letting out a defeated sigh, I grabbed my plate, placed it on the empty cart, and left the dining hall. Perhaps Nana could give me advice on what to do or she could talk to Elder Nehemiah.

* * *

Returning to our room, I found Nana sitting on the couch knitting another scarf. She smiled to me as I sat beside her. "Enjoying your free day so far, dear?"

Glancing down at my hands, I wasn't sure how to begin the conversation about Snow's mom. Nana placed a hand atop of my own. "Is something bothering you?" She asked.

Letting out a sigh, I told her. "Snow's mother hits her."

Nana remained silent. Her hand tightened its grip over mine. Meeting her gaze, I saw a mixture of emotions within her eyes. Pity, sorrow, anger. "I knew Elder Nehemiah was a strict woman. But hitting a child is never justifiable." Nana placed her knitting things on the small table beside the couch and stood.

"Where are you going?"

Approaching the door, she said, "To speak with Elder Nehemiah."

Chapter Nineteen: Saving Snow

"When will you learn?"

I sat on the ground, tears falling from my eyes. My cheek throbbed in pain. My knuckles bled. Snot poured from my nose.

My mother glared down at me. Her lips were curled in disgust. Disappointment flashed within her icy eyes. "I was eating breakfast, *mother*."

Her hand snatched me up by the hair. A yelp of pain sounded from me as she forced me to stand from the ground. Her fist held a clump of my hair. "You must obey your mother. There are no excuses."

Her other hand struck me across the face again. My skin stung in pain. I choked back my tears. "I'm sorry." I managed to say.

Suddenly, a knock sounded at our door. I prayed to the goddess, thanking her. My mother let go of her hold on my hair and stormed toward the door. Swinging it open, I saw Willow's grandmother standing there. Immediately, my mother straightened herself but kept her scowl.

"What do you want?"

Willow's grandmother glanced over my mother's shoulder, her eyes found mine. They widened with shock as she took in my red cheeks, my crying eyes, and tangled mess of hair. Her face hardened with anger as she glared at my mother.

"My granddaughter had a concern about her friend. And I see she had a right to worry."

My mother placed a hand on her hip. "What did the *savior* have a concern about?"

"That you hit your daughter. And I see with my own eyes that this is true." Her voice darkened.

My mother shifted on her feet and slightly began to close the door, blocking me from the old woman's view. "How I discipline my child is none of your business or your nosey granddaughter's."

Willow's grandmother placed her hand on the door. "If a child is being abused then I'll make it my business, Elder Nehemiah."

"You have no proof." My mother's voiced hissed.

The old woman thrust open the door and pushed my mother aside. She strode toward me, her hands gently grasped my shoulders. Her eyes looked me over. I could see pain in her face. Pity. Her eyes wondered down to my hands. A gasp escaped her as she lifted my bleeding knuckles. Her hands gently gave mine a squeeze.

Hardening her eyes, she whirled around and faced my mother. "This," she gestured toward me, "is my proof."

My mother crossed her arms over her chest and raised a brow to the older woman. "And what do you plan on doing? You can't take my daughter; it is not your right. You have no authority here."

Willow's grandmother held her hands behind her back and took a step toward my mother. "Unless you want me to present this issue before the council, I think I'll be leaving with Snow."

My mother's scowl deepened. Her brows creased together causing wrinkles to form upon her forehead. Her lips curled back. "You can't keep her away from me forever."

"Just for a few days but if I ever find that this child is being abused ever again, I *will* bring you before the council."

My mother said nothing more to the woman but she continued to stare her down as the old woman approached me.

"Go gather some clothes together, dear." She spoke kindly to me.

Without glancing toward my mother, I quickly rushed into my room. Frost squeaked as I began to pack a bag of clothes. He scampered up my arm and slid into the pocket of my shirt.

His head tilted back, his red eyes watched me. "I heard what happened. I'm glad someone finally said something to your mother." He spoke.

"Let's just hope that after a few days, when I come back, she won't hit me anymore." My voice trembled. Part of me was scared to leave, what would my mother do when I came back? But another part of me was relieved.

Slinging my bag over my shoulder, I left my room and followed behind Willow's grandmother. For a brief moment, my mother and I's gazes met before I shut the door behind me.

Chapter Twenty: Roommates

Nana returned with Snow. Her blue hair was a mess. Her cheeks bright red with hand marks. Her knuckles wept with blood. Tears dried on her skin. Rushing toward her, I wrapped her in a tight hug. A squeak sounded from her pocket and I took a step back. Frost peaked his head out of her shirt pocket. His beady red eyes staring into mine.

Glancing toward my Nana, I asked, "What happened?"

"Willow, take her to the bathroom and help her wash up." Nana urged us forward. "We'll talk once she's freshened up."

Entering into the bathroom, I turned on the faucet. Warm water poured into the sink. Dipping a wash rag into it, I grasped one of Snow's hands gently and began washing away the blood. She winced when the rag touched her wounds. Apologizing, I dipped her hand into the sink water. When her hands were washed, I rinsed the rag and washed the dried tears and snot from her face. Once she was washed up, I took a brush and began to comb through the tangles in her blue hair.

"Thank you." She whispered.

For a moment, the brush stilled in her hair. "You're welcome." Setting the brush on the counter, I faced her. "Are you alright?"

She bit her bottom lip and her eyes avoided mine. "Yeah, I'm okay. Maybe being away from my mother for a few days will do us both some good."

"Maybe so."

Leaving the bathroom, we returned to the living room. Nana was seated in the red velvet chair beside the couch. She gestured for us to sit. Once we were seated, she spoke.

My Nana's eyes softened as she glanced at Snow. A small smile spreading across her thin lips. "When I visited their room, I heard some unsettling things. When her mother opened the door, I was in shock. So, I took the child away, for the time being."

"How long is she going to stay with us?" I asked.

"A few days." Nana answered me.

Trying to make light of the situation, I snaked an arm around her shoulders, "Well, it's a good thing I have a large bed." I winked at her.

A small smile appeared on her lips.

Nana stood from her chair, "Willow, why don't you and Snow go into your room and help her unpack her things?"

Snow and I left the living room and entered into my room. Salem and Luna greeted us with a chorus of meows. Frost leapt from Snow's pocket and onto my bed. Salem and Luna jumped onto the mattress and greeted her familiar. Opening my closet doors, I pushed all my clothes onto one side of the rod, giving her space to hang her clothing. Then I cleared out a dresser drawer. Snow unpacked her things quietly. Putting her clothes onto hangers and putting them in the closet. She folded pants, skirts, and underwear and placed them in the empty drawer. Once she was done, she let out a sigh. Her blue eyes wondered over to my desk where my half-finished painting lay. Walking toward the desk, she grabbed the painting. A smile spread across her lips as she peered over her shoulder at me.

"So, am I your muse now?"

An embarrassed laugh escaped me. It was a painting of Snow. Her face was half turned toward the viewer of the painting. One of her blue eyes was covered by a piece of white hair that was slowly changing into blue. Her plump lips were pulled into a mischievous smile. "I was going to give it to you once it was finished."

"It's beautiful." Her eyes sparked with happiness. "Perhaps it could be your Samhain gift to me."

"Ah, I almost forgot about the gift giving. My Nana and I would give each other gifts every year."

Carefully, she lay the painting on the desk. "So, have you decided on a dress you're going to wear?"

My eyes glanced over to my closet. "I don't have anything fancy enough for the celebration. Or a mask."

"Don't worry about the mask. The council always has masks prepared for everyone."

"What other big and fancy holidays are celebrated here?" I asked.

"The next one is Yule, winter solstice. That holiday is our next *biggest* celebration."

"Let me guess, there's going to be dancing, correct?"

She smiled, "Of course. Just no masks are needed for that celebration. No evil spirits to confuse." She joked.

"Any other holidays?"

Her eyes broke away from mine. "The day of Ostara." When I didn't speak, she continued, "Though that day symbolizes the last day of winter and the first day of spring. It also was the day that the prophet child was said to be born. So, for five hundred years they celebrated that day in hopes the prophet child would be brought into this world."

"And now, I'm here. Not sure what I'm meant to do."

She chuckled, "Of course you know. End the war between the witches and exorcists."

"But after all that, what am I to do?" So much sadness sounded within my voice. I sat down upon my bed, feeling defeated.

Snow stood before me, holding the painting I had made for

her. "This." Her finger tapped the side of the portrait. "This is what you are to do after you save the day." She handed the painting to me.

I smiled and took the portrait from her hands, "Thank you."

Standing from my bed and walking past Snow, I placed the painting down upon the desk, flattening it out.

"Are you meeting with the Sisters of the Night?"

My smile vanished. "No." I answered.

"You know, you don't have to meet with them." Snow said.

Turning to face her, I asked, "What do you mean?"

A mischievous grin spread across her lips, "Spy on them."

"Why would I want to do that?"

Snow raised a brow as if to say, *really?* "To see what they do at these meetings."

"I don't know about this…"

"You can't tell me that you aren't just the least bit curious about what they do."

"Fine, I'll think about it."

Snow smiled, "Tell me all about it when you get back."

Chapter Twenty-One:
Spying

The clock read eleven forty-five. The meeting would begin soon. Snow, Nana, and the familiars were all sound asleep. I lay on the bed, my eyes staring out the window and into the dark night. The moon was high and full. Shining brightly amongst the stars. Glancing toward the clock again, it read eleven fifty. A silent sigh escaped me. I was curious and I wanted to know exactly what occurred during these meetings.

Glancing over my shoulder, Snow was still sleep. Her blue hair a tangled mess. Carefully, I moved from the bed. My footsteps were silent upon the cool floor. Opening my closet, I grabbed a green cloak and swung it over my shoulders. Slipping on a pair of knee-high black boots, I tucked my wand into my left boot. Slowly, I shut my bedroom door behind me and made my way toward the main door of our room. Nana was nowhere to be found within the living room. Muffled snores echoed from her bedroom. Quickening my pace, I opened the door and slipped into the dimly lit hallway.

Tiny flames danced about upon the wicks of candles. Sconces lined along the walls. The light from the small fires caused shadows to dance about. My body was bathed in a warm glow. All was quiet within the council hall. Not a soul to be found or a noise to be heard. Everyone was sound asleep, except for the Sisters of the Night and I.

Descending down the stairs, the building grew ever darker. Candles were scarcely scattered about, floating along the air. Approaching the massive, double doors, I peered behind me. No one was around. Sneaking outside into the chilly night, I made my way toward the garden. I could hear voices traveling along the wind. Arriving at the garden gate, I saw a gathered group of people before the fountain. They were all cloaked in black.

Quietly, I opened the gate and slipped into the garden, hiding myself behind a rose bush. Peeking through the bush, I watched as one of the people lowered their hood. Fiery hair spilled across the girl's shoulders. Danielle.

"I guess the prophet isn't going to show." Said a random girl.

Danielle glanced toward the gate, "I guess not." Her face hardened with anger.

"Come on, the moon is full. Let's take this into the woods so we don't get caught." Spoke that same girl again.

Danielle turned away from the gate and brought the hood of her cloak over her head once more. "Alright. Let's go."

The group began to make their way toward the gate. Marching along the stone path. Calming my panic, I drew forth my wand. Closing my eyes, I quietly called upon my magic. *"Oh body of mine, morph into the creature of my choosing. The soul and body of a rabbit, I call forth."*

My body began to tingle as my being was transformed. My limbs shrank. My skin grew black fur. Tall ears popped from the top of my head. A small bushy tail twitched. Peering around me, everything was so large now. The rose bush towered over me. The sound of footsteps echoed within my ears. Closer and closer the group came. Soon, they were walking past me, not even taking notice of the little black rabbit. The gate swung open with a creak as the girls stormed out of the garden and disappeared one by one into the forest across the field.

Closing my eyes, I focused on my human form. What it felt

like to have fingers and toes. Walking on two legs. I imagined myself. Long black hair. Two different colored eyes. And the mark upon my forehead. My body began to tingle. It rushed along my spine. I began to grow. The black fur disappeared and was replaced with pale skin. My legs and arms stretched. My black, long hair fell across my back. I was human again.

I hurried off across the field. The grass was dewy beneath my feet. My boots becoming damp. Closer I was coming to the forest. My eyes caught movement within one of the trees. Skidding to a halt, I drew forth my wand. A shadowy figure dropped to the ground from the tree. For a moment, it stood there, watching me. Then, the figure advanced toward me, closing the distance between us. The moonlight bathed the figure in its glow, revealing the white robe the person was wearing. Then, their auburn eyes met with mine.

Anger flared within me. "What do you want?"

The Exorcist said nothing, he soon stood before me. The tip of my wand pressed against his chest. He loomed over me, he was so much taller. A wicked grin appeared upon his lips. "Hello." His voice purred.

Pressing the tip of my wand harder against his chest, I asked again, *"What do you want?"* My voice demanded.

"I wished to pay a visit to my favorite witch."

"Come here to bless me?" My voice hardened.

"Oh, no. That isn't my job."

Taking a step back from him, I said, "Leave."

He cocked his head to the side. "Now, do you *really* want me to leave, Willow?"

"Yes."

He shrugged his shoulders, "Fine. I only came here to tell you about your parents." He turned his back to me and began to walk away, "But if you preferred I leave…"

"Wait." He stopped in his tracks and peered over his shoulder. "What about my parents? Are they alive?"

"Yes." His voice grew serious, "But, you might wish to hurry with whatever plan you have brewing. Or they might end up dead or without magic. Perhaps both."

"How long do they have?" I asked, scared to know the answer.

"A few months, a few weeks. It's hard to say. The Priest never seems to make-up his mind."

"Why are you telling me this? Why does it seem like you're trying to help me, *help a witch*?"

His auburn eyes settled upon me for a moment. His brow creased together. "And that is something I don't have an answer to."

"Liar." I said, still aiming my wand at him.

The Exorcist glanced toward the forest, "You might wish to hurry along before you miss the group you were following." Facing me once more, he crossed the small distance between us with blinding speed. He was so close to me that I could feel the warmth radiating from his body. A smile spread across his lips as he peered upon my flustered face. "Until next time, my favorite witch." With that, he dashed into the forest and disappeared from sight.

* * *

They were gathered in a clearing, circled by trees. A bonfire crackled. The flames casting menacing shadows into the forest. The girls were circled around the fire, their heads bowed. The only part of their face that was visible was their mouths. Their hoods covered their eyes and noses.

Then, one of the girls broke from the formation, stepping toward the fire. "Tonight the moon is high and full," The girl spoke loudly for all to hear, "Tonight, we give to the dead the taste of our blood."

My body stilled. They couldn't be...

The girl lowered her hood, it was Danielle. The other's followed and lowered their hoods as well. "Tonight, we give to the dead our blood. And they will give to us part of their power." Danielle withdrew a long dagger from her black cloak. Holding her wrist above the crackling flames, she brought the blade of the dagger down against her skin. "I, Danielle, offer myself, my blood to other side, the world of the dead." The dagger slid across her wrist. A thin line of crimson appeared. Droplets began to fall into the fire. Black smoke began to rise. A wicked grin spread across Danielle's face. Her eyes shifted color. The brown shade of them vanished and was replaced by crimson.

Danielle stepped away from the flames and returned to her place in the circle. One by one the girls stepped forth and sliced open their wrists, feeding their blood to the fire. More and more black smoke filled the air. Once the last girl had offered her blood, she took her place in the formation. The girls tipped their heads back and gazed toward the dark night sky.

The black smoke lowered to the ground like a thick, dark fog. It swirled beneath their feet. The clouds spiraled up their legs, around their torsos, and entered into their gaping mouths. The clouds lifted their feet from the ground and held them within the air. Their bodies convulsed as the dark clouds entered into them. Their crimson eyes glowed.

This was wrong. So very *wrong*.

Once their bodies had absorbed the dark mass of the clouds, they were lowered to the ground. Danielle spoke again, "For three full moons we have sacrificed our blood and for many more we will continue to do so." Then, withdrawing her wand from her cloak, she spoke, "Now, we must hide our true selves. Mask our eyes with falseness."

The other members drew forth their wands. Danielle closed her eyes and her mouth murmured a spell, *"Oh eyes of mine, transform to a color so none will know of the truth that lurks below."*

The other girls repeated. Their voices sounding haunting. So monotone. It sent chills along my spine. Their voices melded and echoed together throughout the forest. Their eyes began to glow, changing. Shades of browns, greens, and blues covered the girls crimson eyes.

"And for tonight, this meeting is complete." Danielle covered her head with her hood, "Until next full moon."

"Until next full moon." The others said.

The group began to disperse. Breaking from their formation. The fire extinguished itself. The girls were approaching the trees. They would soon find me. Panic took over me. I glanced around the dark forest. Making a move, a twig snapped beneath my feet. My body froze. The group had stopped in their tracks.

Danielle stepped forth and called out, "Who's there?" she began to make her way toward the tree I was hiding behind. I would be found. There was nowhere I could run. What would she and the others do when they found me?

Suddenly, an arm wrapped around my waist and I was flying into the air. A squeal almost escaped my lips until a hand cupped around my mouth, silencing me. We flew into the highest part of a tree and landed upon a branch. The hand around my mouth turned my face so that I may see who had captured me. The Exorcist was smiling wickedly. His auburn eyes staring into mine. Removing his hand from my mouth, he brought a finger to his lips. *Shhh.* He nodded his head toward the ground. There Danielle was, standing where I had been hiding just moments ago.

"Everyone, search this forest. Someone followed us tonight. No one can know about this. *Go!*" She ordered. The girls began to disappear into the dark forest. They were on the hunt, for me.

The Exorcist leaned close to me, his lips brushing against my ear, "Seems that you have gotten yourself caught." He whispered.

"They don't know it was me." I whispered back.

A quiet laugh escaped him, "Because of me, of course. Otherwise you would have been found. I do wonder what they would have done to you." His breath was warm against my cool skin. "I believe you owe me a thank you."

"I owe you nothing." I snapped.

"Fine. Since it seems as though you don't need my help." He released his hold around my waist. My body was falling. My arms flailed about, my hands reached and tried to grasp the branches that passed me by as I fell. Closer and closer the ground grew. My eyes met with auburn. There he sat upon the branch, watching me as I fell. I couldn't scream, the group of blood witches would hear. Locking with his gaze, my mouth muttered, *"Thank you."*

A pleased smile spread across his lips as he leapt from the branch. His arms were stretched toward me. He scooped me into his arms and we flew into the night sky. The wind whipped my long, black hair about. Making it a tangled mess. My arms wrapped around the Exorcist's throat, tightly out of fear of falling. Plummeting to the ground. The wind pushed back the white hood of his robe, revealing his dark brown hair. Our faces were so close to each other. I stared into his auburn eyes, counting the few scattered golden flecks within his irises.

The corners of his lips twitched into a smile. His brow raised. "Enjoying the view?"

"There's not much to view." I turned my face away from his.

He chuckled. "Your mouth might say that, but your eyes seemed to disagree."

I rolled my eyes. "Whatever."

"You still owe me a proper thank you."

"I did thank you."

"I wish to hear you say it instead of your lips remaining silent."

A groan escaped me.

He turned his gaze toward me and raised a brow. "Unless you prefer to fall to the ground, that is." His hands loosened from around me.

"Thank you!" I squealed as I clung to his neck.

His arms tightened around me. He laughed, "Now, was that so hard?"

"Ass." I muttered.

Together we flew over the forest, the trees racing below us. The wind ripped through my hair and I'm sure it smacked the Exorcist in the face a few good times. He spoke not a word until we reached the end of the trees. We lowered to the ground. My feet landed upon the dew covered grass.

"I would have taken you closer to the Council Hall but I don't need the gargoyles alerting every one of my presence. That would make things rather difficult." Stepping away from me, he said, "Goodbye, Prophet. Until next time." He winked as he disappeared into the forest.

* * *

I was able to sneak through the building without anyone spotting me. It was still late into the night. When I returned to Nana and I's room, the sound of her snores filled the silence. Stepping inside my room, I found snow sitting upon the bed. Her legs crossed together, her arms crossed over her chest. Her blue hair a tangled mess.

"And what did this spy see?" She asked.

The door clicked shut behind me. I contemplated whether or not I should tell her the truth. Tell her what I had witnessed. "Don't lie. I can tell that you're trying to think of way to avoid telling me the truth."

My brow raised.

Snow chuckled, "I know because I do the same thing to my

mother. So I know when someone is about to lie right through their teeth." She patted the bed beside her, "Tell me."

Removing my cloak, I returned it to its hanger in my closet. With a sigh, I seated myself beside Snow. "I found Danielle and her coven, group, whatever, inside the garden. Then, I followed them into the forest across the field." Snow's brow raised. "They were in a clearing," I left out the part about the Exorcist, "They were circled around a bonfire. Danielle stepped toward it and grabbed a dagger from her cloak." At this point, Snow's face had drained of color, "She sliced her wrist and blood dripped into the fire. She said it was a sacrifice to the dead so that she can gain power. Once everyone had done that, their eyes turned crimson and they used magic to mask the color."

Snow blinked a few times, not knowing what to say, trying to process what I had just told her. She shook her head, "I knew Danielle was a horrible person but I never would have thought she would be a… blood witch." She whispered the last words. "You do realize that we have to tell the council."

"Yeah, if they believe us. Danielle is Elder Darrio's daughter."

"Then I'll tell them." Nana was standing at the door. How long had she been there?

Suddenly, I realized something. "Wait. If they get blessed, then they'll…" I couldn't say that word.

Nana approached the bed and sat beside me, her hand resting atop mine. "I know. It saddens my heart to see so many young girls leave this earth. Perhaps they'll find the light and welcome the goddess into their souls once more." She placed a kiss on my forehead, "Now, get some rest."

Chapter Twenty-Two: Blessing of the Blood Witches

"And do you have proof of this accusation, Anora?" Elder Artemis questioned Nana.

"In order for blood witches to gain power from the dead, what must they do?"

Elder Artemis leaned back in his chair, his fingers rubbing his chin. "Slice a part of their body to draw forth blood." Glancing over at Elder Darrio, he said, "Bring your daughter here."

Elder Darrio said nothing, remaining silent. Slowly, he stood from his chair still holding Elder Artemis's gaze. His shoes sounded against the floor, echoing around the quiet room. The doors closed shut behind him.

A little while later, he returned with Danielle. His hand tightly grasped her arm. Her dark eyes met with mine. So much spite, so much hatred shot toward me. It was then she knew that I was the one in the forest last night.

Elder Darrio and his daughter stood before the council. Elder Artemis rose from his chair, "Now, Danielle, there are claims against you. Claims that you are a blood witch. Is this true?"

Anger flared within her eyes as she shot another glance toward me. "Of course it's not true." She snapped.

Elder Artemis held up a hand, "Calm your anger. If you wish to prove your innocence then I ask of you to push up the sleeves of your shirt, please."

Danielle tensed. Her body stilled. The flames of anger burning within her eyes disappeared, blown out like a tiny flame on a candle. Terror showed itself upon her face. Elder Artemis looked upon her, he knew. There was no point in her pushing up the sleeves that covered her arms. But she must to prove to the rest of council, to her father, that she was indeed a blood witch.

Danielle wiggled free of her father's hold, stepping away from him. He turned his black eyes upon her. "Do as he says." His voice was low.

"No. I'm innocent! She's lying!" She screamed as she jabbed a finger in my direction. "Liar!" She stomped her foot, tears began to fall from her eyes. She knew what this meant. Death.

"Do as he asks, Danielle!" Elder Darrio grabbed his daughter and pushed up the sleeve on her arm. The room was enveloped by silence. The air seemed to still. No one spoke a word. The council's eyes were upon the father and daughter. Elder Artemis lowered to his seat.

"Why?" Something broke within Elder Darrio's eyes. His heart. He couldn't understand why his daughter would turn against the light and venture along the path that led to the dark.

Danielle snatched her arm away from her father. A bloody gauze was wrapped around her wrist. She could have healed it. But we were taught not to rely on our magic for everything.

"I'm sorry, Darrio." Elder Artemis addressed him without title, he addressed him like a person, like a friend. Like a man that was about to lose his daughter. He glanced toward Elder Arya, "You know what must be done."

Her emerald eyes were wet with tears. She would be

ending the lives of many girls. She nodded her head. "Bring the other girls."

"No!" Danielle screamed. "Father you can't let them do this!" Elder Darrio avoided eye contact with her. "I'm your daughter! They'll kill me!"

"You knew this would happen." He said with so much sadness sounding in his voice.

A look of betrayal crossed her face. She took another shaking step back away from her father. "So you're going to let them kill me? You're only child?"

Elder Darrio did not answer her. "I'll fetch the other girls." He said before he left the room.

"Dad!" She cried out after him.

And I could have sworn I saw a tear fall from his dark eye.

* * *

He had returned with the other girls. Each of them lined up before the council, Danielle standing before the group. Elder Artemis nodded his head to Elder Arya. Letting out a saddened sigh, she stood from her chair and approached Danielle.

"Please…" She pleaded to Elder Darrio. "Dad…"

The man closed his eyes and shook his head. His hands were clasped together, his knuckles turning white.

Danielle turned her crying eyes to the elder woman that stood before her. "I'm sorry." Elder Arya said as she pointed the tip of her black wand toward Danielle.

Elder Artemis turned his attention to the broken man. "Do you wish to say any final words to your daughter?"

Elder Darrio glanced toward the floor and very briefly at his daughter. "No."

Elder Artemis nodded his head. "Elder Arya." He gave the order.

As she began to chant the spell, something occurred to me.

I remembered from one of my lessons with Elder Arya.

* * *

"Elder Arya, I thought I was the only witch with a connection to the veil? When I entered into it I could see a thin line of connection coming from your body."

"You are the only one who can enter into it. The only one with a direct connection. All witches power stems from the veil but none of us can see it. None except you. And since you have that connection, if an Exorcist were to bless you with their purification power then their power would stream into your line of connection straight into the veil. And once their purification enters into it, then it shatters."

"When I was in the veil and saw your connection, I reached out for it but something inside of me told me to stop. Can I sever other witches connection from the veil?"

"Yes." She answered me with stern eyes. *"If you are not careful you can sever the link between a witch and their magic."*

* * *

"Wait!"

Everyone's attention was upon me. Elder Arya ceased her spell casting and turned her emerald eyes upon me.

"What is it, Willow?" Elder Artemis asked.

Approaching the council members, I said, "There's something I can do. She and the others don't have to die."

The council members regarded me with disbelief. "What can you do?" He asked.

Glancing at Elder Arya, I said, "I can enter into the veil of magic and sever their links to it."

The room grew hushed once more.

Elder Artemis turned his attention to the other council

members. Each of them nodded their heads. "So that no one has to die on this day, and so that no parent has to suffer the loss of a child, we agree to this, Willow. Severe their links."

"You can't!" Danielle cried. "Just kill me! I don't want to live without magic!"

"Silence, child!" Elder Darrio's voice roared. "The prophet is willing to save your life. Do not be stubborn."

Danielle hushed her protests and turned her dark eyes upon me. "This is all your fault to begin with." She said in a low voice as I approached her.

"I didn't force you to become a blood witch."

"Just, get it over with." She closed her eyes.

Focusing upon my connection to the veil, I followed my link. My essence gliding along it, the silver, glittering line leading me. The magic roared and burned within my veins, my body thrummed. A burning flame dwelled deep within my being, crackling and sizzling with power. A warm sensation caressed my body, crawling along my skin. Then, an explosion of light enveloped me. When I opened my eyes, the world before me was encased with magic. Shimmers and glimmers of magic floated about within the air around the room. So colorful it was. Sliding my gaze toward Danielle, I saw the magic within her veins. But it was not bright, filtering with light like Elder Arya's did. It was dark, cursed, bloody. It moved slowly within her body. And though her eyes were closed, I could still see the bright crimson color of them through her eyelids. Looking above her head, I saw her connection to the veil. It was just as dark as the magic within her veins was. My hand slowly lifted toward her connection. Her eyes fluttered open and stared into mine. A chill tickled my spine. Never shall I forget the color of her crimson eyes. Breaking my gaze away from hers, my fingers touched her link to the veil. It seemed to hiss at me, refusing to leave her body. I knew it was the evil that tainted her. Forcing my fingers through the connection, it separated from her being. No longer did magic flow within her veins. No longer did her crimson eyes stare upon me. They had returned to their natural, dark color.

Her familiar flew into the room. The raven glowed with magic. Glittering blue specks raining from its body. Its wings flapped, sending shimmers scattering about within the air. It landed upon her shoulder. She didn't look upon the raven.

"Danielle?" Its female voice called out her name.

A single tear rolled down Danielle's cheek. The raven hung its head. "Then, this is goodbye, my witch." The raven nudged its head against her cheek. Before it flew away, its eyes landed upon me. "Thank you for sparing her life, savior. It is my time to leave her and join the side of another witch." It glanced toward the silent Danielle. "She can no longer hear my words." With a flap of its wings, it left the room and Danielle.

A witch no longer stood before me.

She was now a human.

Chapter Twenty-Three: Magicless Lives

Weeks have passed since the day I severed Danielle's and the other girls link to the veil. Weeks since they were forced to live magicless lives, forced to be human. I thought I had saved them but really, I gave them a life without magic. A life where they no longer knew who they were. What their purpose was. Out of all the girls, Danielle took the loss of her magic the hardest. She was but a shell, hollow and empty. No longer did she make snide remarks at Snow and I. She walked with her head held low, her gaze to the floor. There was not a sign of the old Danielle to be found. I had broken her.

Snow and I were seated in the dining hall, eating our breakfast. Danielle entered into the large room pushing a cart of fresh food. She had taken to kitchen duty with her mother after what happened. Now, she barely spoke to her father and barely casted a glance my way. Danielle pushed the cart against the wall and rolled the empty one out of the room.

A sigh escaped me as I turned around and continued eating my breakfast. "In a way, she kind of deserves this." Snow said.

My fork stilled, "No one deserves to be broken. Not like that."

"She was asking for it, Willow. She knew that by being a blood witch something would happen. She's not stupid." She rested her chin on her hand, "I wonder what made her convert."

Glancing toward the doors, I said, "I don't know."

* * *

Later that day, while wondering about in the hallways, I bumped into Danielle. Mostly on purpose. I wanted her to make a comment, to be rude, just *something*. Instead, she mumbled sorry and stepped around me.

"Wait." I called after her. She stopped but didn't face me. "What... What made you convert?"

For a while she stood there, not speaking a word. And I began to think she would never answer me until she breathed a heavy sigh and peered over her shoulder. "Why do you want to know?"

"I don't understand why you did it."

Turning her face away from me, she said, "It doesn't matter anymore." With that, she walked down the hallway and disappeared around the corner.

"I'm sorry." I said aloud but I knew she didn't hear me.

* * *

Returning to my room, I found Snow, Nana, and Erin waiting for me in the living room. Frost sat upon Snow's lap. Salem and Luna were laid across the back of the red couch. And a snake was wrapped around Erin's shoulders. Its slit pupils were focused on me. Its forked tongue flickered from its mouth. A chill crept along my spine. I have never been fond of snakes. Part of its scaly green body slithered across his left shoulder, its head close to Erin's ear.

"Have you guys come up with a plan?" I asked as I seated myself beside Snow, far away from the snake.

"No. we're just having a meeting; to see how much you have learned." Nana said. "What has Elder Arya taught you?"

"So far all I know is shapeshifting magic and elemental magic."

Nana nodded her head, "There is still much for you to learn, Willow. We cannot save your parents until you have more knowledge about magic. Knowing only a few spells won't help you when we go against the Exorcists."

Feeling useless, I rested my head within my hands. I wanted so badly to go and rescue my parents. I couldn't imagine what they were going through at the hands of the Exorcists. How long did they have until they were killed or left without magic? How long?

A hand gently placed itself on my shoulder, "Willow, you'll get your parents back. I promise." Snow said tenderly.

"I hope we won't be too late."

"They took your parents as a trap. They won't harm them; they need them to lure you." Erin said.

Nana let out a sigh, "It is true what he says." She turned to me and lay a hand upon my knee, "Don't worry. We will get them back."

* * *

Once again, I was roaming the halls. Not to find Danielle but to have some alone time. My parents were trapped, prisoners, and as of now there was nothing I could do to save them. Glancing down at my hands, I couldn't help but think, what was the point of being "powerful" if I couldn't even save my parents? If I was so *"powerful"* then I wouldn't need to learn so many spells before we could go and save them.

"Hello, Willow." Lifting my head, I saw Elder Arya standing before me. "Are you alright?"

Shaking my head, I admitted, "No. I'm not alright."

Arya stepped beside me and wrapped an arm around my shoulders, "Come."

She led me down the hallways and into the scholar room. The candles lit a flame and danced about within the air. Elder Arya motioned for me to sit at the table. Taking a seat, she sat beside me.

"Tell me."

Finally, I broke. Tears swelled within my eyes. My hands trembled. "I hate being the prophet. I *hate* it." My voice cracked. Elder Arya placed a warm hand over mine. "My parents were taken by the Exorcists because I'm the prophet. They could die because of who I am. They're probably dead already." Tears began to stream down my face, dripping onto Arya's hand. "And then, I took away those girls' magic. Danielle isn't the same. She's just empty. And I had done that to her. *I* had broken her."

Elder Arya wiped away my tears. "Willow, you saved those girls' lives. If you hadn't have severed their connection, then they would have been killed."

"I might have saved them, but I gave them a life without magic. Some of them probably wish they were dead."

"They brought this upon themselves, Willow. You spared their lives when they were about to die, by my own hand. Because of you, now parents won't have to mourn the loss of a child. *Because of you*, they are alive."

She stood from the table and walked across the room. When she came back, she handed me a few tissues. I thanked her and began to wipe my eyes and nose. "Feel better?" She asked.

I breathed in, "It felt good getting that off my chest."

She smiled sweetly, "Good. Erin let me vent to him many times after the loss of our parents. It helps."

"When can we start our lessons again?"

She looked concerned, "Are you sure you're ready? I've given you some time off with all that's been happening."

"Please, I'm ready."

She patted my hand, "Alright, tomorrow morning we begin our lessons."

* * *

Nervously, I knocked on the wooden door. Footsteps approached and the door swung open. Elder Nehemiah scowled at me. "She'll be out in a minute." Then, she slammed the door in my face.

"Thanks..." I slumped against the wall, waiting for Snow.

A little while later, Snow emerged from the room, carrying a bag slung over her shoulder. "Sorry to keep you waiting. Mom wouldn't stop talking." She rolled her eyes.

Glancing toward the door, I asked, "Are things okay?"

"Ever since your Nana threatened to tell the council, she hasn't been as... angry." She smiled, "Plus staying with you a few nights a week helps, both of us."

Snow looped her arm through mine and we began marching down the hall to my room.

"So, my lessons with Elder Arya start tomorrow. Might have to eat breakfast without my company unless you want to starve until I get back."

"Don't worry, I'll be asleep until you get back." She laughed.

"I'm just ready to learn more magic so we can start making a plan to save my parents."

Snow glanced around us and held a finger to her lips, "Wait till we get to your room to talk about stuff like that." She whispered. She glanced around again, "But keep me updated with your lessons."

"Will do."

Chapter Twenty-Four:
Lesson with Elder Arya

"Today, you'll be learning how to summon lightning."

Elder Arya stood from the chair she had been sitting on, waiting for me to arrive for our morning lesson.

I raised a brow, "Why didn't you teach me that with the other elemental magic?"

"I was going to teach you, the day after you learned fire and earth. But, I gave you those free days so you could rest."

"Oh."

Elder Arya smiled and approached the window. Aiming her wand outside the opened window, she began to speak. *"Oh, the most striking force, lightning, this form of nature I summon forth!"* The tip of her black wand ignited with a bright light. Then, lightning shot forth into the sky. Storming into clouds. Turning to me with a smile on her face, she said, "Now, you try. Remember to disconnect your emotions from your magic."

Elder Arya stepped away from the window. Holding my wand outside, the cool air licked my skin. Closing my eyes, I disconnected my emotions and summoned my magic. *"Oh, the most striking force, lightning, this form of nature I summon forth!"* The tip of my wand sparked at my command. Lightning crackled and stormed into the sky.

"Good." Elder Arya said with a smile.

"What's next?"

She raised a brow, "You seem eager to learn lately."

I shrugged my shoulders, "There's not much else to do around here."

She regarded me for a moment before she spoke, "Alright. One more lesson for today." Holding her wand before her she said, "This next spell will prove to be very useful and might even save your life." She closed her eyes and spoke, *"Oh magic of mine. Come forth and protect me from harm's doing."*

Wisps of foggy air streamed from the tip of her wand. They wrapped around her being, forming a shield. The barrier was a solid force of air. "Try to reach me." She said. Stepping toward the barrier, I reached my hand out to touch it. I soon found myself being denied from coming near the Elder woman. A smirk crossed her lips. "Now, you try." Elder Arya called back her magic and the wall of wind dispersed.

Holding my wand, I closed my eyes and repeated, *"Oh magic of mine. Come forth and protect me from harm's doing."* Spirts of foggy air flooded from the tip of my wand, spiraling around my being. Incasing me in a wall of wind. A barrier.

"Good, Willow." Elder Arya spoke.

Releasing my magic, the wall of wind dispersed. The Elder woman approached me. Her fingers swept aside my bangs. "A few more details have showed themselves in your mark. Has anyone questioned you about this?"

My bangs fell across my forehead as she stepped away. "No. My bangs keep it hidden well enough I guess."

She raised a brow, "Willow, your mark extends across your cheekbones now, everyone has noticed."

"No one has said anything to me about it, not even Nana."

A sigh escaped her, "Because we all knew that would happen once you began unlocking more of your magic, learning more. It was also foretold in the prophecy."

"What's the point of all these markings?" I questioned her.

Arya sucked in her bottom lip, biting it. She shook her head, avoiding my gaze. "It wasn't much explained. Just to mark you as the goddess's chosen one." I felt as though, she was hiding something from me. But, what?

"What hasn't been told in the prophecy?" I sighed. "So, I guess there's no point in having bangs anymore." I said, trying to make a joke out of this.

"Your Nana cut your hair like that to hide you away from Exorcists while you were living in the human world. Now, there is no longer any point to it, they have seen your face. They know the prophet is here." She stepped toward me and cupped a warm hand around my cheek, "If you wish to fix your hair, then do so." She smiled.

"You know, I have to admit, I hate having bangs."

Elder Arya laughed, "But, they suit you well."

"What's the lesson for tomorrow?" I asked.

Elder Arya winked an emerald eye. "You'll see." With that, she left the scholar room and me behind.

Letting out another sigh, I stepped toward the still open window. My arms leaned against the sill. The wind playfully rustled my hair, sweeping aside my bangs. The air kissed my mark as if the goddess herself had placed her lips upon my forehead. Gazing into the clear sky, my lips whispered, *"Why have you chosen me?"*

* * *

Standing before the bathroom mirror, my eyes examined the mark upon my forehead within the reflection. Swirls and twirls danced along the curving, black lines upon my cheekbones, lacing together elegantly. My mark was turning into a tiara that was permanently etched into my skin. A mark that was also a target for the Exorcists.

My fingers traced along every curve, every swirl that extended from the opening of the crescent moons. Above the center moon, the full one, was a dot. Sprouting from the dot were two spiraling lines that curled into themselves. A dot placed into the space that separated each line. There were several little dots scattered throughout the mark. They curved along every twirling line, filling in every empty space. It was like my skin was a canvas and the mark was the paint, the masterpiece.

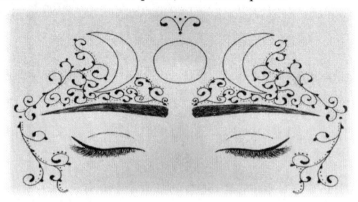

I began to wonder; just how many markings would appear on me? Would the moons become completely black? Then another thought emerged within my mind; after the Exorcists have been destroyed, would the mark disappear? Was that foretold in the prophecy as well?

No one really told me *exactly* what was foretold in the prophecy. The only things I know is that the goddess chose me and I was destined to bring the war between the witches and the Exorcists to an end. I needed to start asking questions.

* * *

The halls were empty, not a soul to be found. It was still early into the evening; dinner would be served soon. I could smell the meal the kitchen staff was preparing. Chicken, tomato soup, buttery rolls. My stomach growled with hunger. My mouth began to water at the delicious scent.

Venturing down a hallway, the candles lit the way. Someone had closed the currents over the windows, blocking out the sun's light. My feet walked along the plush, crimson carpet that stretched along the length of the hallway. Candles danced about above my head. Twirling within the air. The sound of a door closing echoed within the hallway. A figure slowly approached. Their black cloak trailing across the ground behind them. A raven was perched on the person's shoulder. Closer and closer the person came. Then, the candle light illuminated the person's face. The Elder man's black eyes settled on me.

Elder Darrio stood before me, staring me down. "Hello, prophet child." His voice was dark.

"Hello." My voice was quiet.

His familiar regarded me but remained silent.

"Why are you roaming the halls?" He questioned me.

I fumbled about, trying to find my words. "Because I'm looking for answers."

The Elder raised a dark brow. "Answers to what?"

"The prophecy."

"What are you wanting answers to?"

I avoided his piercing gaze. "All I know about the prophecy is that I'm supposed to end the war between the witches and Exorcists."

"Then that's all you need to know." He brushed past me. "Don't bother asking anyone else, savior. No one will tell you."

I whirled around, angry. "Why is everyone hiding this from me! I need to know!" I yelled, frustrated. I was tired of people hiding things from me. Things that involved *me*.

Elder Darrio stopped in his tracks. The raven turned its eyes upon me. The Elder spoke in a way that sent chills along my spine. "The prophecy is never to be told to the prophet. You must never know what truly lies within it. You are told only what you need to know and nothing more. No matter who you ask, no matter how many times you ask, you'll never receive the answers you're searching for, Willow." With those final words, he disappeared down the hall. The raven keeping its eyes upon me as the Elder walked away.

* * *

"I'm sorry, I wasn't told much about it either, Willow." Snow answered with an apologetic look on her face.

A groan escaped me as I fell onto my bed, face first. "I don't understand." My words were muffled by the blanket.

"I'm sorry, girl. Just don't stress about it, you already have enough to stress about." Snow said.

"Thanks for reminding me." I muttered. I turned over on my back, staring at the ceiling. "After my lesson with Elder Arya tomorrow, we will start forming a plan to save my parents."

"We'll leave that decision to your Nana."

Another groan.

Snow leapt off the bed, "Alright miss grumpy pants, get up." She tugged on my feet. "Up! Up! Up!"

"Where are we going?"

"I am getting you out of this room and outside." She tugged on my feet more, dragging me down from the bed. "Up!" With one last tug, my body fell off the bed and landed on the hard floor.

I was too busy bursting out into laughter to pay any mind to my hurting ass. Snow was crippled with laughter, falling to the ground beside me. "Well, you have successfully dragged me off the bed. Where else are you going to drag me?"

Snow wiped away the tears from her eyes, "The garden. You usually go there when you want to clear your head."

"Then, to the garden we go."

* * *

Snow and I seated ourselves on a bench before the fountain. Though the sun was shining brightly, the air was cool against my skin. "Summers here aren't very warm." I said.

"The Elder's keep out the heat from the sun during the hotter months. Plus, it is late August now. Two months until our Samhain celebration." Snow grew giddy with excitement. "Gosh, I can't wait. Do you know what color dress you want to wear?" She asked.

"Hmm. I haven't really given it much thought." I glanced over at my blue haired friend. "I'm guessing you're going to wear blue?"

Her lips formed into a smile, "How did you guess? It was my hair. A dead giveaway." She giggled.

The gate door creaked open behind us. Peering over my shoulder, I saw Elder Nehemiah waltzing toward us. Her blue eyes were focused upon her daughter. "Snow, it's time for your lessons." She briefly glanced toward me, her eyes grew wide as she spotted my mark, but said nothing.

"Alright, see ya later, Willow." Snow scurried off behind her mother and I was left alone in the garden.

"Well, so much for that." I muttered under my breath.

So quiet it has been around here lately. It seemed as though barely anyone lived in the council hall anymore, like people had just disappeared without a trace. As I was sitting upon the bench, gazing into the clear sky above me, there was a rustle within the tree beside the fountain. Grabbing my black wand from the inside of my boot, I stood from the bench.

"Who's there?" I called out.

Then, I felt a presence behind me. "I think ruby would be a suitable color on you." A voice whispered into my ear.

Whirling around, I came face-to-face with the auburn eyed Exorcist. He cocked his head to the side as his eyes studied me. "Your mark has gained some new, interesting details."

"What do you want?"

He raised a brow as he leapt onto a high tree branch and crouched on it. "Just to deliver some news regarding your parents, Willow."

My breath stilled. My heart thumped within my chest. "What about my parents? Are they alive?"

"Very much so, I'm sure you are glad to hear."

"Anything else?" I pressed on. Trying to get more information from him.

"They still have their magic. But your parents have been separated, moved to different cells. A form of torture, I guess." He propped his elbow on his knee and rested his head in the palm of his hand, "Which will make it more difficult for you to rescue them."

"Have you told the Priest that I'm planning on rescuing my parents?" I pointed my wand to the Exorcist.

He barked out a laugh, "Oh, silly prophet, that's exactly what he wants. For you to go running right into his trap."

"Then why even bother coming here to talk to me?"

His auburn eyes regarded me for a moment before he leapt down from the branch and stood before me. My wand pressed into the center of his chest. "Perhaps because I wish to be free, just like you wish to be."

I took a step away from him, "What do you mean?"

He advanced toward me, "The council has you trapped here, correct? And if you succeed in ending the war between us, then you'll be locked here forever, which is also correct, am I right?"

I shook my head, "Stop talking."

He raised his brows, "Oh? So you don't like hearing the truth?"

"Stop." My voice was a low warning.

"Why don't you just runaway, Willow? You could right now if you wanted too."

"What? Runaway with you? Is that what you want?" I laughed, "You'd just bless me the second you had a chance. You'd be the hero of the Exorcists. They might even bump you up to Priest for killing the prophet witch." My words sounded with so much harshness and hatred.

    He glanced at me for a moment before he took a step away. "What we have in common, savior, is that we both wish for a life of freedom. A life to make our *own* choices." He leapt over the fence and glanced over his shoulder, "A ruby dress would suit you, Willow." Then, he disappeared into the forest.

Chapter Twenty-Five: The Ruby Dress

I had found this in the garden laid across a marble bench. A note was set upon it. I am glad I found this before anyone else could.

A ruby dress for Samhain. Enjoy, Willow.

The dress was elegant. The ruby was rich and deep with color. Black sequins lined along the top portion of the dress where my breasts would be. There were no sleeves to it, instead it would cling to my chest. The skirt was crafted with lacey, black ruffles. They would sweep across the floor, fan out around me as I danced, if I danced.

I began to wonder where and how he acquired the dress. There was a knocking upon my bedroom door. Quickly I slid the note underneath my pillow as Snow entered into the room. Her blue eyes landed on the dress that was stretched across the bed.

"Is that the dress you're wearing for Samhain? It's beautiful." Her fingers trailed across the ruby fabric. "I thought you said you didn't have a *fancy* dress?"

"Well, uh, I didn't think this was fancy enough for the celebration."

She raised a brow and nodded toward the dress, "Trust me, it's fancy. Now, did you not go to morning lessons today?"

"I did. But Elder Arya wasn't in the room and I couldn't find her anywhere."

Snow smiled, "Perhaps you weren't looking hard enough."

* * *

I had wondered the halls for an hour, still no sign of the elder woman. Pushing open the door to the scholar room, the candles danced about. Glancing around, there was not a soul to be found. With a groan, I slumped down on a chair.

"Where are you?"

The door clicked shut, the sound of footsteps echoed within the room. But there was no one to be found. Withdrawing my wand, I aimed it before me. The sound of giggling laughter filled the room. My heart began to race with panic.

"Who's there?" I called out frantically.

There was no answer. Closing my eyes, I focused on my connection to the veil. My magic began to thrum within my being, flowing through my veins. Opening my eyes, the world glistened with iridescent colors. Focusing before me, I saw the silhouette of a cloaked person. Their being was transparent. A link to the veil streamed from their body.

"Who are you?"

The person turned to face me. The woman's lips tugged into a smile. "Clever, entering into your connection of the veil to find me." Elder Arya spoke.

"You were hiding from me?" I asked.

She chuckled, "It is part of your lesson today, Willow." Her being began to shimmer brightly and she was no longer transparent.

Closing off my senses to the veil, the glittering world fell away, "Invisibility?"

She raised a brow, "So, you are familiar with this magic?"

"Not really, once before Nana used it to hide us in a human

town. But I couldn't remember the spell she used."

Nodding her head, she said, *"Oh magic of mine, come forth and hide my body from wondering eyes."*

Closing my eyes and holding my wand, I repeated those words. Peering around me, I saw that glittering, currents of air spiraled through the room. Circling around my body. The magic wrapped itself around my being, infusing into my skin. Then, I had disappeared from sight. Even I couldn't see my own limbs.

"It'll be a little disorientating at first, since you can't see your own body. Take careful steps, Willow."

As I began to take a step forward, I stopped. "Wait." I said, causing her to glance at me curiously. "If I enter into the veil, then I'll be able to see myself, like I saw you."

A smile of pride spread across her lips, "Clever you are."

Focusing on my connection to the veil, the world burst into color around me. Glancing down at my hands, I saw the ghostly outline of them. Taking a step forward was easy now that I could see my legs and feet.

"You never cease to amaze me, Willow." Elder Arya said with a sweet smile.

Closing off my senses to the veil and calling back my magic, I spoke to the elder woman, "It's nothing too amazing."

"You may think so, Willow. But many others agree with me. Now, tomorrow, you are free. I have some things to prepare for Samhain. Enjoy your day." With a smile, she left the scholar room.

* * *

Glancing into the mirror, I viewed myself wearing the ruby dress. It fitted well to my body, complimenting it. The ruby color went along well with my pale skin. My black hair matched with the sequins. The skirt fanned out around me as I twirled around a few times. The lacey, black ruffles wisped about along the air. If I closed my eyes, I could imagine myself dancing at the Samhain celebration. The music filtered through my ears and echoed within the room. A ruby mask with black sequins disguised my face, my mark. And in that moment I would be no one. I wouldn't be the prophet child. I wouldn't be the savior. I would be me and I would be no one. For a night, my worries would disappear.

    Closer and closer the celebration was drawing near. With a sigh, I unzipped the back of the dress. It fell from my body and pooled by my ankles in heaps of ruby and black fabric. Stepping out of it, I grabbed the dress from the ground and placed it back on its hanger and put it in the closet.

    Glancing outside, the day had gone. Hours had passed since my lesson with Elder Arya. The night had brought itself upon the world. Sleep was calling to me. Crashing onto my bed, I drifted off into the land of dreams.

* * *

The cool morning air licked at my cheeks. The sun had dosed the land in its warm, orange glow. All was quiet in the garden except for the sounds of splashing water in the fountain. My paintbrush stroked across the paper, leaving streaks of colors behind. I had decided to finally paint the garden before the winter claimed it. The leaves were already beginning to brown. The rose bushes on the paper I had painted bright red, some of the others I had painted a creamy white. Brown roots grew from the grassy ground, holding the trees into the earth. The fountain had spurts of glistening, clear water shooting from the top of it into the air. The picture was blossoming with colors. Taking form. A smile of pride flashed across my face. My heart burned with passion, a passion for painting. Perhaps after the war is over, I could do this professionally, like Snow suggested.

    "Beautiful." A voice whispered into my ear, startling me.

My paintbrush fell from my hand and red paint splattered across the stone pathway.

Grabbing my wand from a belt loop on my pants, I whirled around and found myself face-to-face with the Exorcist. "What do you want?"

His auburn eyes glanced upon my painting that lay across the bench, taking in every painted detail, every stroke of the brush. "A true talent you have, Willow." He said.

"Thanks."

He faced me with a brow raised, "So now I don't have to beg for you to thank me?"

Glancing behind him, I checked to make sure no one was watching. "You need to leave." My voice was stern.

He closed the distance between us and wrapped an arm around my waist. "What are you doing?!"

He leaned down and whispered into my ear, "Going someplace where we won't be seen."

Without waiting for me to protest, we took to the sky, soaring through the clouds. The wind whipped my hair from its ponytail, freeing it. My body shuddered as the cold air nipped at my skin. My eyes watered. The Exorcist tightened his arms around my shuddering body. My cheeks flustered.

We lowered down in a small clearing, trees circled around us. The Exorcist's arms were still wrapped tightly around me. Those auburn eyes of his stared down upon me. "Did you like the dress?" He asked.

Breaking free of his arms, I said, "Yes. But you shouldn't have done that. What if I hadn't of found it?"

He smiled mischievously, "Oh, I knew you would find it."

"Thank you."

"Another thank you? I'm beginning to think that you like me, Willow." He winked an auburn eye at me.

Rolling my eyes, I said, "No, I don't. We're enemies."

"We don't have to be." His voice sounded with such

seriousness.

"You know I'm destined to end the Exorcists."

"I suppose so."

As he stood there, the wind caused his white robe to drift along its currents. His brown hair brushed away from his warm eyes. Standing there, he seemed so… lonely. Lost. And for a moment, I had forgotten what he was. The tattoos of crosses on his hands disappeared from my sight, his white robe vanished, and what was left was a teenage boy close to my age that seemed so alone in this world.

"Could you stop being an Exorcist?" I found myself asking.

His auburn, golden flecked eyes fixed on me. "No, Willow."

"Why?"

He took a step closer to me. "Because, I have no choice."

"Were you told to kill me? The day you found me in that town, were you supposed to kill me then?"

He did not answer.

"You made a choice that day and even now, not to kill me."

"What makes you think I didn't bring you here to kill you? No one would hear your screams. It would be quick and easy." He was close to me, so close. I could feel the heat radiating from his body. His eyes stared down upon me.

Meeting his gaze, I said, "You won't."

His brow raised. "Oh, you think so?"

I straightened my back. "Yes, I do."

In an instant, he had me pinned against a tree. A hand around my throat but I could breathe with ease. As I stared into his eyes I found that I was not afraid. I did not fear him. And I knew he wouldn't kill me.

"So easily I could snap your neck." He whispered.

"But you won't."

His auburn eyes met with mine. The Exorcist's body was

so close to mine, our faces just mere inches apart. Our noses almost touching. I found my gaze wondering down to his lips.

"Putting your trust into an Exorcist, your enemy, how foolish can you be?"

Hardening my face, I said, "And how foolish are you to come here to a place where hundreds of witches live?" I demanded to know why he frequently visited here, visited me. "Tell me why."

The look in his eyes told me he knew what I meant. His gaze wondered across every inch of my face. His hand moved away from my throat and grasped a strand of my midnight hair. "Because, I no longer feel alone."

My heart ached at his words.

"Both of us live a life where we are never given a choice. Everything is decided for us. Our pasts, presents, and futures have all been decided and will be decided." He whispered, "And that is why I am drawn to you."

My heart thumped at his words. "Is that the only reason?" I faintly voiced.

Those auburn eyes of his fixed upon my lips, his thumb traced along my bottom lip. Then, they met with my gaze. "No." He answered.

"Then tell me the other reason."

His brows creased together as he tried to decide whether to voice his true reason or keep it a secret. "I can't tell you."

"Why not?" I pressed for an answer.

Our gazes met, "Because you are the prophet and I am an Exorcist. We both know how this will end."

"Then why bother visiting me? Why go through the trouble?"

A sigh escaped his lips, "I can't seem to stay away."

"It can't be that hard."

"Every time I have visited, you could have walked away but you didn't."

My gaze broke away from his but his hand cupped around my cheek, forcing me to look at him. "You have trouble staying away too." His voice whispered.

"Maybe I do." And I found myself shocked when those words escaped me. And I could see that the Exorcist was shocked as well.

The warmness in his eyes faded away as we both realized what needed to happen. He wrapped his arms around me once again and we took to the sky. We flew in silence, the wind whispering to us, filling the silence. We lowered down in the garden and the Exorcist released his hold on me.

"This is goodbye, Willow." The Exorcist said.

"Before you leave, what's your name?"

He turned his back to me, "Learning my name doesn't matter anymore."

"If this is goodbye then I want to say goodbye to *you*."

A sigh escaped him, "Elrick."

"Then, goodbye, Elrick." It felt strange saying his name. *Knowing* his name. For so long all I knew him as was the Exorcist. Now, learning his name felt so… personal. Like this simple name drew us closer together.

Elrick didn't look back as he took to the sky and disappeared into the clouds.

Chapter Twenty-Six: Duel

A few days had passed.

"Today your lesson will be outside." Elder Arya said. "And it will be different. You won't be learning anything new but I will be testing what you know."

Following the elder woman outside, we found ourselves in the field before the forest. Elder Arya took a few steps back, putting distance between us. Drawing forth her black wand, she aimed it at me. "Draw your wand, Willow."

Doing as she asked, I grabbed it from my left boot. "What exactly are we doing?"

She smiled, "A duel."

My brows raised, "Me against you? An elder?"

"I'll only do spells that you have learned so far, Willow. Don't worry."

"But you're an *elder*."

"And you're the prophet. Both of us are strong but you are stronger than me." She paused, "Now, ready yourself. Here's my first attack."

My palms began to sweat.

"Oh the most striking force, lightning this form of a nature, I summon forth!" Lightning manifested. It crackled through the air and raced toward me across the field.

My heart thundered within my chest. Quickly, I began to call upon my magic. *"Oh magic of mine, come forth and protect me from harm's doing!"* My voice was shaky but my magic did as I commanded. A wall of wind encased me. Lightning struck at the barrier, unable to reach me.

Elder Arya called back her magic and the lightning disappeared. "Good. Now you attack me."

"Oh fiery form of nature, I summon you forth!" A streak of blazing fire shot forth from the tip of my wand.

Elder Arya smiled and began to summon her magic. *"Oh fiery form of nature, I summon you forth!"* Flames ignited from her wand and stormed toward me. Our fires met with one another in the center of the field. A blaze scattered across the grass. Sizzling fires rose into the air, devouring the ground.

Elder Arya and I summoned back our magic and the fires dispersed. "Now it's my turn." She said. *"Oh earth beneath us, this form of nature, I summon forth!"*

The ground rumbled beneath my feet. Vines sprouted from the ground. They danced within the air around me. The vines latched onto my body, wrapping around my arms and legs. I was held captive. Glancing down, my wand was still tightly grasped within my hand. *"Oh fiery form of nature, I summon you forth!"* Fire burst forth from my wand, engulfing the vines. The flames devoured the plants, freeing me without injury.

Elder Arya waited for my next attack, a smile of pride flashed across her face. *"Oh purest form of nature. Water, I summon you forth!"* From the fountain, water rose into the air. It rippled along the wind, making its way toward the elder woman. The water formed into waves, rising high and touching the clouds. Bringing my wand down, the waves crashed toward Elder Arya.

Acting quickly, she summoned upon her magic, *"Oh magic of mine, come forth and protect me from harm's doing!"* Within an instant, a wall of wind surrounded her and the water slammed against her barrier of magic. None of my attack reached the elder woman. The water crashed onto the ground creating a large mass of water around the wall of wind encasing the woman.

Both us called back our magic. The water returned itself to the fountain within the garden. Elder Arya's barrier dispersed.

Without warning, she began to summon upon her magic, *"Oh wind of nature, I summon you forth!"* The wind around us whipped through my hair, tangling it. The air circled, spinning, faster and faster. The wind blew me back, knocking me off balance. It howled within my ears, roaring. I braced myself against the strong currents of wind. But harder and harder it pushed against me. My feet slid across the ground, uprooting the grass beneath me.

Holding tightly onto my wand, I called upon my magic, *"Oh earth beneath us, this form of nature I summon forth!"* Vines sprouted from the dirt and wrapped themselves around my legs, stopping above my knees. I was rooted in place, no longer could the wind knock me off balance.

"Very clever, Willow." Elder Arya said with a smile. "Your turn."

Going through my memories of lessons with Elder Arya, I choose my next attack, *"Oh the most striking force, lightning this form of nature, I summon forth!"* Pure white lightning thundered forth from the tip of my black wand. It crackled and danced within the air as it raced across the field toward the elder woman.

Elder Arya summoned lightning as well. They collided together. An explosion of magic burst into the air. Glitters of magic danced through the air, shimmering as they disappeared before landing upon the ground.

"What happened?" I asked.

With a smile of pride she said, "That means, Willow, you are stronger than me."

"But how?" I asked in disbelief.

"The greeting of the elders is way to determine who is strongest. And though what just happened wasn't the greeting, it still means the same. Your magic is stronger than mine which caused the lightning to burst."

Glancing down at my hands, I still couldn't believe it. I was stronger than an elder. Elder Arya approached me, "But there are still spells for you to learn. Though you might not have enough time to learn them all before you save your parents."

My gaze met with hers, "How did you know?"

She winked an emerald eye, "I am no fool, Willow. I would be planning to save my parents if I were you."

"Are you going to tell the council?"

"Of course not. I'll be helping you on your mission to save your parents."

My eyes widened, "Really?"

"Yes. Is there anyone else joining you?"

"My Nana, Snow, and your brother."

She smiled, "I knew my brother would help you. But we cannot save your parents immediately though it saddens me to say. Wait till after Samhain and I promise, Willow, we will get them back."

"Thank you, Elder Arya."

Her hand cupped around my cheek, "Of course. Now your lesson for today is finished." Turning her back to me, she returned to the council hall. Her black robe rippling across the currents of wind.

* * *

Sitting on a marble bench, I waited. Silence surrounded me, mocking me. The cool air nipped at my skin, trying to persuade me to leave the garden. A voice echoed within my mind, telling me he would not come back. Asking me why I even bothered waiting. My focus was upon the forest across the empty field. I hoped that the Exorcist would appear, leaping from a tree or walking out of the darkness. A sigh escaped me, I was a fool to think he would return. And I was even more foolish to allow myself to care for my enemy. Standing from the bench, I turned my back to the garden and left.

* * *

There she was, sitting alone on a bench. Her two toned eyes stared into the forest. The wind gently breezed past her, tendrils of midnight hair wisped into the air. Waiting, she was waiting for me. Something tugged at my heart, something told me to go to her, but my body remained still. So much regret dwelled within me the day I told the prophet goodbye and walked away from her life. But we both knew that this was the way it must be. She was a witch, the *prophet*, and I was an Exorcist. We were enemies, even before either of us were born, we were destined to fight one another. Gazing upon her, I knew that I could never raise a hand against her, even if the Priest demanded I do so, I would refuse and suffer the consequences.

  Willow stood from the bench, cast one last glance into the forest, and turned her back to the garden, to me. Leaping down from the tree branch, I was so tempted to run to her but my feet remained stilled, rooted in place. This was for the best, I kept telling myself, though I found it hard to be true.

  Once she disappeared from sight, I flew into the clouds, leaving Willow far behind.

Chapter Twenty-Seven: Dancing with the Enemy

The day had arrived. Samhain. The council hall was bustling. Hurried people rushed through the halls. Kitchen cooks prepared mass amounts of food for the celebration. The air was coated in scents of baking pastries. Pumpkin pie, I noticed, stood out more than the other smells.

Black candles danced above my head, swirling about within the air. The white ones had been switched out for the celebration. Pumpkins were scattered about; holes had been cut in the center of them allowing the candles light to shine through. Black ribbons had been tied around the stems of the pumpkins.

Wooden tables had been lined along one wall, black table cloths covered them. Crimson details laced through the dark fabric, almost like a spider web. Silver platters and utensils were placed atop the tables. Soon, food would be brought out and placed onto the platters. My stomach growled as the smell of cooking food wafted into the air once more.

Lanterns hung low from the ceiling, a warm glow emanating from them. The candles were careful not to bump into the lanterns. The room had a warmth to it, an autumn glow. It wrapped around my being, encasing me with its welcome of warmth and chill. The air grown colder but with autumn came the feeling of warmth from fires. Glancing out the window, I saw leaves scattered across the ground. Hues of reds, oranges, yellows, and browns. The trees were barren, their branches stripped of their green leaves. Almost seeming like skeletal hands reaching for the sky. I had decided I wanted to go outside and paint the scenery. Though summer and spring were lovely seasons to paint, they didn't share the same feeling as Autumn and Winter.

Gathering my painting supplies, I headed outside toward the garden. The gate door moaned as I pushed it open and once more when I closed it behind me. The fountain steadily sounded with splashing water as I approached it closer. When I came to my usual bench, I stopped. My breath caught in my throat as I eyed the mask that lay upon the marble. Ruby it was with black feathers that fanned out from the eyes. My fingers reached for the creamy slip of paper beneath it. Shakely, I unfolded the note and read it.

A mask to match your dress.

The Exorcist, *Elrick*, had been here. I remembered his writing from his last note. Lifting my gaze from the note, I peered around me, hoping to find the Exorcist. But there was not a soul to be found, I was alone here. My hope died as I turned my attention back to the mask. It would match well with my dress but part of me felt there was no need to wear the outfit. No need to join the Samhain celebration. With a sigh, I scooted the mask aside and set to work on my new painting.

"Hello, Willow." A voice spoke from behind me, startling me. Whipping around, with wand in hand, I came face-to-face with Danielle. Her dark eyes wondered down to my wand, pain flashed across her face.

Putting my wand in the back pocket of my jeans, I said, "Hey."

"You wanted to know why I converted." She said, her eyes not meeting mine. "I'll tell you." It was then I realized the dark circles blossoming beneath her eyes, deep and purple. "I wanted to be stronger than you. Ever since you arrived here all I heard was how you could save us and end the war. How you were the prophet. Then when I learned you had a connection into the veil, I thought you'd have a connection into the other world, too."

"That's why you wanted me to join your group."

She nodded her head, "All I wanted was to be stronger and better than you, maybe then people would stop talking about you. But, that'll never happen."

"You converted into a blood witch, just so you could be stronger than me?"

"Sounds stupid, I know." Her eyes finally met with mine, "I knew what would happen if I got caught and part of me was hoping for death. You should have let me die." Her words sounded with anger. "What kind of life is this?" She stretched her arms out, "A witch turned human because her magic was taken from her? You might as well should have killed me yourself." The old Danielle was slowly coming back. "You enjoyed taking my magic from me! You wanted to be the only witch everyone talked about! It's all about you!" She cried out as she lunged herself at me. Stepping aside, she fell to the ground in a heap of cries.

Lifting herself onto her elbows, her gaze met with mine, "Please… give me my magic back."

Shaking my head, I said, "I can't and I'm sorry."

She turned her face away from me, "People say you can do anything, and you refuse to give me my magic back."

"I can't do anything and I can't give you your magic back. Your connection was cut from the veil, I'm sorry, Danielle."

"Some prophet you are." Though her words sounded with spite, there was a hint of sadness, despair lingering within them. "Just, leave."

I said nothing more to her as I gathered my painting supplies and left the garden.

* * *

    The dress and mask were laid across my bed. The crimson, black fabric falling from the edge of the bed and sweeping across the floor. Opening my closet door, I searched through my shoes to find a pair that would match the dress. Grabbing a pair of black, ankle boots with thick, chunky heels, I placed them on the bed. A sigh escaped me as I glanced toward the clock. The celebration would begin soon.

    Grabbing the dress, I began to change into it. Pulling it up to my chest, I zipped up the back. Sitting on the edge of my bed, I slid my feet into the ankle boots. Then, I held the feathered mask within my hands. The feathers felt silky against my skin. It had been weeks since Elrick and I said goodbye. Weeks since we left one another's lives. A sickening feeling dwelled within my stomach as I realized something. When we go to rescue my parents, he will be there. Will he fight against me? Will we have to fight one another? A sigh escaped me as I tried to push that thought from my mind.

    Standing from my bed, I approached the mirror. My reflection stared back at me, my emerald and auburn eyes watching me. My hair fell down to my waist in midnight waves. No longer did I have straight across bangs, I had allowed them to grow out. Now my hair was perfectly parted down the middle. Bringing the mask up to my face, I tied the black ribbons together. The dark feathers expanded past my face. The mask surprisingly hid away my mark. Tonight, I would be no one. Grabbing my wand from my nightstand, I hid it away in my ankle boot. Then, I hurried out of my room and down the stairs toward the celebration.

    The entry room was filled with masked people. Women wore dresses of all colors and styles. The men wore black tuxedos with different colored ties that coordinated to the falling leaves in autumn. Candle light danced about within the room.

The black candles floated above the people's heads, the pumpkins lined along the walls, some set in the center of the food tables. The lanterns offered their own warm glows as they hung from the ceiling. Soft music filtered through the air. The sounds of violins and flutes humming their enchanting music.

It was easy to spot Snow in the crowd of masked people, her blue hair bounced with curls. Her dress was beautiful. A deep blue that shimmered with every turn she made. It was silky and tight fitting to her body. The dress cascaded down her body and pooled by her feet in waves of blue. Her mask matched with the dress. Deep blue with black lacing around the eyes. A smile lit up her face as she talked to the person beside her, Erin. His tie matched her dress, which they probably planned to match. And just like every other man in the room, he wore a simple black mask and tuxedo.

As I entered into the room, the music slowly began to fade away and the room was enveloped in silence. Everyone turned their attention toward the group of people that entered. The elders. Each of them wore a black dress or tuxedo. The women's midnight dresses shimmered in the candle light. Their masks were feathered, even the men's. I noticed the golden haired man, Elder Artemis in front of Elder Arya. Her brunette hair was straightened and fell down to her lower back. The elders lined up in front of the gathered people. In unison each elder drew forth their wand and held them within the air. Spheres of light emanated from the tips of their wands and danced within the air, spiraling around one another. Twirling. Higher and higher they rose until the lights were above the group of masked people. Then, they collided. Glitters of magic twinkled within the air as they drifted down and showered upon the people, upon me. They wisped along the ground and disappeared from sight.

Elder Artemis stepped forward, "Tonight we celebrate Samhain. The end of warmer months has come and the beginning of cooler months approach. These coming seasons bring an end, death, to many things. Tonight, the veil between worlds draws thin, tonight the dead can walk amongst the living. Tonight we wear masks to confuse those of the otherworld. So until dawn rises, we must be careful, never wonder alone outside. And never remove your mask." His voice sent chills along spine, "Now, enjoy Samhain." He clapped his hands together and the music began once more.

The group of people separated, men and women partnering together to dance. Erin offered his hand to Snow causing a wide smile to spread across her lips. Placing her hand in his, together they danced. His hand rested on the lower of her back as their bodies were drawn close together. They swayed to the enchanting sound of the flutes and violins. Spinning and twirling around the room, alongside the other dancing couples. Snow's happy laughter sounded through the air, her blue eyes twinkled as she stared upon Erin. A sweet smile formed on his lips. My heart ached within my chest as I watched them dance together happily without worries consuming them.

With a sigh, I ventured over to the food tables. The smell of freshly baked pumpkin pies surrounded me. My stomach growled as it caught the scent of the pie. Approaching the table, a fiery haired woman smiled to me. "Hello," She spoke. "Is there something I can help you with?"

"I just want a slice of pumpkin pie, please."

Her dark eyes glanced toward the warm pie, "Allow me to cut you a slice." Grabbing a plate and knife, she cut a small piece and placed it upon the plate. "Here you go."

Taking the plate from her hand and grabbing a fork, I said, "Thank you." Then, everything pieced together in my mind. The fiery hair, dark eyes. This was Danielle's mother.

Stepping away from the food tables, I leaned against a wall and ate my pumpkin pie. It was warm and delicious. It danced across my taste buds. Peering around the room, people still danced together and I suddenly felt so alone. Smiles were painted across everyone's faces, happiness beaming from them. Glancing down at my empty plate, I didn't notice the stranger that approached me.

"What's a beautiful woman like you standing here alone?" Their deep voice sounded within my ears.

Glancing up, a masked man stood before me, "You don't even know what I look like beneath this mask."

The person leaned close to me, "But, I do."

"Do I know you?"

He chuckled, "Maybe, maybe not." Offering his gloved hand to me, he said, "Would you like to dance?"

Peering at the other people dancing, I slid my hand into his, "Yes."

The masked man led me across the room and into the center of the dancing people. His hand slid across my waist and rested upon my lower back, his other hand still holding gently onto mine. He drew my body close to his. Our faces were just mere inches from each other. We began to sway along to the sound of the violins and flutes. The music guiding our movements. Removing his hand from my lower back, he spun me around. The room twirled as he spun me back into his arms. My heart raced as his heart beat beneath my fingertips.

"The dress suits you, Willow." He spoke.

"Thank you." My voice was barely a whisper. Glancing up, I tried to find out who this person was, if I knew them. Gazing into the holes of their mask, I tried to see their eye color but the dimness of the room made it hard to see. "Who are you?" I found myself asking.

A mischievous grin formed upon his lips, "Soon, you'll figure it out." His hands rested upon my hips, "For now, let's dance."

One of his hands slid down to my lower back while the other rested upon the center of my back. My hands found themselves behind his neck, his dark hair brushed against my skin. So warm he was, so close we were. Our noses inches apart.

"How do you know who I am?" I questioned him.

"Everyone knows who you are." He answered.

Then, a candle drifted past us, the tiny flame doused us in a warm glow and I could finally see his eye color. A gasp escaped me as I stared into that warm, golden flecked, auburn color. "Elrick?" My voice whispered.

The Exorcist smiled, "You remembered my name."

It had been so long since we last saw one another. Since the day we both said our goodbyes. "Why did you come back?" I glanced around frantically, "Why did you come *here*?"

His hand cupped around my cheek, "Calm yourself. No one will notice who and what I am."

"How can you be so sure?"

"The mask and gloves."

I found myself leaning into the palm of his hand, so warm. "You shouldn't be here, Elrick."

"Did I ever tell you that I like it when you speak my name?" His auburn eyes glimmered.

A smile formed upon my lips, "No."

His thumb moved to trace along my bottom lip. "Well, I do."

My heart thundered within my chest. My cheeks flustered. "Let's go outside, where you won't be surrounded by hundreds of witches."

"Alright." Keeping one hand on my lower back, we slipped outside into the chilly night air.

Approaching the garden, the gate creaked as we entered. The grass had browned, most of the plants had withered away. The trees were barren, their leaves scattered across the ground colorfully. But still the fountain ran, water spurting from the top of it and spilling over its circular levels into the last one, the pond. Elrick stood beside me, his hands reached toward his mask.

"Wait."

"What is it?"

"We were told not to remove our masks."

He gestured around us, "Do you see any ghosts?"

Glancing toward the ground, I said sheepishly, "No."

Elrick removed his mask and took a step closer to me. His hand reached toward me, his fingers set to work untying the ribbons of my mask. It loosened and fell from my face into the palm of his hand. The night air licked at my skin. It gently breezed through my midnight hair.

A smile brightened Elrick's face, "So beautiful." He said.

"Why did you come back?" I asked him again.

He sighed as he combed his fingers through his dark hair. "Because, Willow, I missed you."

Part of me wanted to confess that I missed him as well. "That can't be your only reason." I found myself stupidly saying.

A wicked grin crossed his lips as he stepped closer to me. Taking a few steps back, I bumped into a tree. Elrick braced an arm against the trunk, pinning me in place. "So, you didn't miss me?"

I broke my gaze away from his. "I hardly noticed you were gone."

His fingers tilted my chin up, making me meet with his warm auburn gaze. "Don't lie, Willow." He whispered into my ear, "I saw you waiting for me to come back."

Anger flared within me. "So you saw me waiting and you still didn't come back?"

"Ah, so you did miss me after all." He smiled.

"How many times did you come here? Before tonight."

A sigh escaped him, "Several. Sometimes you would be out in the garden, other times you were nowhere to be found. I was so tempted to approach you and…" He stopped.

"And?"

His auburn eyes met with mine, his hand rested upon my cheek, "And do this." Leaning toward me, his lips brushed against mine. They were so soft. Our lips danced together, melding. He pressed me against the tree, his hands gripped my hips. His mouth devoured mine. Hunger fueled him as did the want of another, the want for me. The kiss held longing, passion.

Two enemies kissed beneath a tree.

Two people fighting on different sides of a war.

Two people who found each other in chance.

Two people who knew what the outcome would be.

Elrick broke the kiss, his lips leaving my mine, as did his warmth. His hands remained on my hips, his breathing was heavy. "I'm sorry." He said.

"You don't have any reason to be sorry."

He shook his head, "I forced that kiss on you."

My hand cupped around his cheek, "I didn't mind it."

His eyes met with mine as his brow raised, "Really?" His face came closer to mine. I could feel his breath against my skin. "Would you like another?" He purred.

"Sounds tempting." My voice sounded with temptation.

Without another word spoken between us, his lips crashed against mine. His hands gripped my hips harder, with hunger. His tongue slipped inside my mouth and danced with mine. A flame of passion ignited within my chest, burning brightly. The taste of him filled my mouth. His lips were moist against mine. I pressed my body against his, the warmth of him surrounding me. My fingers tangled themselves in his dark hair. My heart thundered within my chest. And I could feel that his did as well.

Breaking free from the kiss, I caught my breath. For a moment, we stared into one another eyes. I found myself getting sucked into the beauty and warmth of his gaze. My fingers brushed against his cheek, he leaned into the palm of my hand.

His brows creased together as he closed his eyes, "I hate this." He whispered into my palm.

"Hate what?"

"Being enemies."

Placing my other hand on his other cheek, I forced him to meet my gaze, "*We* aren't enemies." I told him.

"But our people are." He let out a sigh, "And when you come to rescue your parents, there will be a fight."

"Will you fight against me or with me?"

He leaned his forehead against mine. "I'll never fight you, Willow."

"And I'll never fight you."

His eyes gazed into mine as his hand rested upon my cheek, "You are my only weakness." He confessed, "The only person that could be used against me. The only person I care for."

"Elrick, promise me that you won't be anywhere near the fight. Promise me."

He shook his head, "I can't promise you that, Willow."

"Why not?"

He broke away from my hands, "I will be forced to fight. And if I beg to be left out of it, then the Priest will know why and use you against me."

I stepped toward him, "How could he use me against you?"

His auburn eyes were filled with worry, "He can threaten to kill you, even though he already plans on it, he could make it so much worse knowing that I care for you, the prophet child." His fingers twirled a piece of my midnight hair, "I'll sooner die than allow him to lay a hand on you."

I was lost for words. Elrick would go against his own people, his own *leader,* for me. Suddenly, the gate door moaned as it was pushed open. Laughter sounded within the air. Quickly, Elrick wrapped his arms around my waist and we flew into the night sky and into the forest. Just as we were flying away, blue hair glowed in the moon's light. A mask-less Snow smiled to Erin as she removed his mask. Delicately, he brushed a strand of blue hair behind her ear and leaned in for a kiss.

Elrick and I landed on the highest branch in a tree. His arms holding firmly onto me. "This might be the last time we see one another before you attack." He said.

"I plan to rescue my parents in a few days. Be expecting me."

He smiled, "Be sure to ring the doorbell before you storm inside. Politeness is always appreciated."

"Of course." I pulled myself into his embrace and whispered into his ear, "Goodbye, my favorite Exorcist."

Elrick placed a kiss upon my cheek, "Goodbye, my favorite witch." We swooped into the air as he carried me into the center of the field and set me down. "Until next time." He winked an auburn eye and disappeared into the darkness of the forest.

Chapter Twenty-Eight:
Rescuing Willow's Parents

"I'm sorry, but you must remain here." Nana spoke to my familiars.

"But it is our duty to protect, Willow." Salem and Luna said in unison.

Kneeling before the couch, I spoke to them, "I know but I can't risk your lives. Please, stay."

Both black cats hung their heads, "Fine, we'll stay." Their yellow eyes met with mine, "Come back safely, our witch."

I scratched behind both of their ears, "I promise I will."

Snow approached the couch and set her familiar beside mine, "Frost, you stay too."

"I won't argue, just know I don't agree with this." His nose twitched.

"You too, Pya." Erin set his snake familiar across the back of the couch. The snake's green scales shone in the light. Her forked tongue flickered from her mouth. She said not a word, only nodding her head to Erin.

Nana turned her attention toward me, "Now where is she? We'll have to leave in a few minutes, with or without her."

As if on cue, there was a knock upon the door. It opened to reveal Elder Arya and a wolf trailing just behind her. "Sorry I'm late, council business held me up." The large, white and grey wolf stood beside the elder woman. Its icy blue eyes were locked upon me. Elder Arya placed a hand atop her familiar's head, "This is my familiar, Mala." The wolf nodded its head, to me.

"She'll be staying here with your familiars. Now, what's the plan?" She seated herself upon the chair beside the couch.

"Well, obviously we can't travel on foot to the "Church"," Snow put air quotes around the word, "We'll have to take brooms."

Elder Arya snapped her fingers as she thought of an idea, "*Or* we can ride gargoyles. They can also help us fight."

"Excellent idea." Nana nodded her approval. "The question is; how do we leave without alerting everyone?"

Elder Arya glanced toward the clock, "We'll have to leave later than planned. Midnight."

"Because everyone will be in their own rooms and hopefully asleep." Nana said.

Elder Arya nodded her head. "So now, we wait two hours."

I turned to face Snow and Erin, who were holding hands. "You guys don't have to go. I don't want you risking your lives."

Snow let go of Erin's hand and stepped toward me. Her finger poked me on my forehead. "Well, guess what? We're going, whether you like it or not, worry wart."

"So there's nothing I can say to make you change your minds?"

"Nope." Snow crossed her arms, "So stop asking, Willow. We're doing this because we want too and we want to help *you* rescue your parents."

A sigh of defeat escaped me, "Fine."

"What exactly is the plan when we get there?" Erin asked.

"Well, it should be obvious. Storm inside." Elder Arya said.

"And how do we know where it is?"

Elder Arya smirked, "Every elder knows where their home is, brother."

"If every elder knows, then why haven't any of you tried to destroy them before?"

A shadow cast itself across the elder woman's face,

"Because, it was not part of our destiny." Her emerald eyes glanced toward me, "That is for the prophet, she is the one to end them. *All* of them."

My chest tightened, my heart ached. *All* of them had to die. Even, Elrick, the one Exorcist that worked his way into my heart. The one Exorcist who wasn't given a choice in life. Glancing down at my hands, I questioned myself, I couldn't kill them all, could I? My hands clenched into fists, my knuckles turned white. One, I could save one. *My* Exorcist.

* * *

The time had come. The clock struck midnight. Salem and Luna meowed their protests about staying behind, but still I did not change my mind. The other familiars weren't happy about our plan either, but eventually they gave in and remained in the room.

Quietly, we slipped out of the building without being seen. Elder Arya led the way to the stone pillars that lined around the building. Gargoyles rested atop each pillar. Raising her wand in the air, she began to call upon her magic, *"Oh stone guardians awaken, an elder summons you forth!"*

The pillars began to tremble as the gargoyles awakened. Half of them stirred from their deep slumber. Their stone wings fanned out as they stretched their limbs. With a leap, they landed upon the ground before us with a heavy *thud*. The earth shook from their weight. Their stone eyes blinked at the elder that stood before them.

Arya whirled around to face us, "Pick your gargoyle."

Snow hurriedly ran up to one and crawled onto its back, her hands gripped its long, stone horns atop its head. "This is going to be way better than riding brooms."

The rest of the group climbed onto a gargoyle. The stone beast huffed out a breath as I seated myself on its back. My hands gripped its horns. The gargoyle's tail thumped onto the ground as it swayed about. It stretched out its wide wings, eager to take flight into the night sky. It clawed at the ground, uprooting the dead grass beneath us.

"Let's go rescue Willow's parents!" Elder Arya called out as she signaled for the gargoyles to take flight.

The stone guardians raised their wings and with a strong flap, they leapt into the sky. The cold air whipped my hair behind me, freeing it from its ponytail. My eyes watered as the wind breezed against my face. The council hall shrank beneath us as we climbed higher into the sky. Above me, seeming so close but still so far away, the stars twinkled. My hand reached for them but grasped nothing but cool air. Elder Arya led the group of gargoyles toward the Exorcists home, the church.

It seemed like we had been flying for an eternity until a massive structure emerged from the darkness of a forest. A cathedral like building stood tall amongst the clouds. The white marble of it shone with the moon's light. Tall, color stained windows lined along the walls of the building, depicting their god. And at the very top of the structure was a tall cross. There was an eerie feeling about this place, it was too quiet. Silence cursed this place, enveloped it. Not a sound was to be heard, as if the animals had disappeared from the forest without a trace.

With a wave of Elder Arya's hand, the gargoyles dropped from the sky and landed upon the ground before the cathedral. Each of us leapt down from the stone guardians we were seated on and gathered together.

"I'll have part of the gargoyles storm inside, followed by us, and the rest of them will be right behind our group. We'll be protected from the front and back." Elder Arya said.

Nana stood by my side and squeezed my hand, "Willow, no matter what happens, know that I love you."

"I love you too. But we will make it out alive." I said.

Nana smiled and placed a kiss upon my forehead. "As long as you make it out alive, my dear, that's all that matters."

Elder Arya drew forth her wand, "Alright everyone, this is it. Draw your wands and prepare yourselves."

Snow and Erin glanced at one another, he cupped his hand around her cheek and placed a kiss upon her lips. My heart ached watching them. It was so easy for them, both of them fighting on the same side in a war.

"It's time." Elder Arya signaled for part of the gargoyles to storm inside. They charged forward and crashed through the doors. *"Let's go!"* With wands aimed forward, onward we charged.

Beams of light flashed within the cathedral. Our feet passed over the threshold. My eyes took in the scene that was laid before me. Gargoyles flew through the air, chasing after Exorcists. The stone guardians behind us growled as enemies approached us from the sides, boxing us in. Claws clicked against the marble floors as the gargoyles charged at the Exorcists, whipping their stone tails at them. Growls echoed through the massive room, blasts sounded, bits of walls falling apart as the guardians dodged attacks.

Suddenly, a gargoyle leapt in front of me. A beam of light crashed into its stone body, bits of rocks fell from it before the stone guardian fell apart in front of me. Stone pieces scattered across the floor at my feet. The creature had given its life to save mine. The Exorcist that had killed the gargoyle, stood across the room with a smirk written across her face. The crosses on her hands glowed brightly, ready to unleash another attack.

My knuckles turned white as I gripped the wand. I would avenge the gargoyle. Aiming my wand toward the smirking Exorcist, I summoned upon my magic, my anger fueled it. *"Oh fiery form of nature, I summon you forth!"* My magic burned within my body, coursing through my veins. Elder Arya warned me to disconnect my emotions from my magic, but this is when it felt strongest, when my emotions fueled it. Sizzling flames shot forth. They crackled through the air, dancing crazily across the room. They roared and grew in size. The smirk faded away from the Exorcist woman's face. Her wide eyes took in the flames that charged toward her. There wasn't enough time to dodge the attack. A scream of agony sounded from her as the flames devoured her body. She rolled about on the ground, trying desperately to put out the fire. But there was no saving herself, she would die. Soon, her screams had died away as her soul left this place.

The first person I have ever killed. And she wouldn't be the last, either.

Shouts sounded from behind me. Whirling around, I watched Snow and Erin take on three Exorcists. Lightning thundered from her white wand and paralyzed an Exorcist, a gargoyle finished him off. Erin summoned upon earthly magic, causing vines to erupt from the floor. They whipped around the room, encasing Exorcists in their trap. The enemies struggled against the vines, their hands began to emanate their holy light and blasted through the tangle of earth.

Elder Arya and Nana were a force to be reckoned with, together they stormed through the room unleashing magical attacks. Fire and lightning roared from their wands, knocking down enemies, burning and paralyzing them. Shouts and screams echoed around the room like a chorus. Beams of holy light shot toward the duo. Acting quickly, Elder Arya summoned a barrier to protect them. The Exorcists beams slammed into their wall of wind, it never reached the two women.

A growl sounded from above me, glancing up, I saw a gargoyle take aim at an Exorcist across the room. The enemy had raised their hand against me, their cross glowing. The Exorcist let out a cry as the stone guardian tackled them to the ground and demolished their body. Turning away from the gruesome scene, I saw Snow and Erin cornered. A group of Exorcist pinned them against the wall, each of their hands aimed toward the young witches.

Hurriedly, I rushed to their aid. Panic danced across Snow's face. Fear began to consume her. They were cornered, doomed, she believed. Erin firmly grasped her hand, putting on a brave face for her. Aiming my wand at the enemies, I called upon my magic once more, *"Oh wind of nature, I summon you forth!"*

A strong breeze wisped through the room, blowing around like a fierce force. I imagined a gust of wind carrying the Exorcists away, slamming their bodies into a wall. And the wind did just as I wished. Shouts of surprise rang out through the room as they flew into the air, their bodies crashing against a wall. The stone spider webbed behind them, cracks raced through the white marble. The Exorcists slumped to the ground, lifeless? I couldn't tell.

The blue haired witch let out a sigh of relief. "Thanks for the save, Willow."

"Maybe we should stick together in a group." Erin suggested.

I nodded my head in agreement, "We need to find my parents."

Snow gestured around the room, "Almost all the Exorcist in *here* are dead. There's no telling how many more we'll run into before we find your parents."

"Do you really think just the five us can save them?" I dared ask.

"We do have the gargoyles, Willow." Erin said.

As I gazed around the room, I noticed that their numbers had dropped. Pieces of stone and dust scattered along the floor. "So many of them have fallen already." I said grimly.

Snow placed a hand on my shoulder, "Willow, we can't really talk right now, ya know we are in the middle of a fight to the death."

"Then let's finish this." Together we entered back into the fight. And it seemed as though more Exorcists had found their way into the battle.

Elder Arya and Nana were still holding their own, putting up a strong fight. But we couldn't let them fight alone forever. Calling upon my magic, lightning screeched from the tip of my wand and slammed into an Exorcist's body. They fell to the ground, their body convulsed, their limbs twitching. A gargoyle saw its chance and took it, smashing the enemy's head. Bile rose in my throat as I turned away from the scene.

"There's too many of them." Erin spoke to his sister.

"We *can* do this, brother."

"Look out!" Snow cried.

A beam of light was shooting our way. Each of us leapt out of its path. My foot slipped from beneath me and I went tumbling down to the ground. My wand was knocked from my grasp and it slid across the marble floor. There was an Exorcist above me, she smiled wickedly. I tried to get on my feet but she was on me in an instant. Her hands glowed. Those crosses dangerously close to my face. My hands grasped her wrists, pushing them away from me. My gaze locked on the crosses, my heart thundered within my chest, my pulse raced. Sweat began to form upon my brow. Fear began to claw at my skin. So brightly her hands glowed. And a single touch could mean the end of all witches' magic, *forever*. Their fate lay on my shoulders.

Glancing around, I found that I was alone. There was no one to help me. Down the gargoyles fell one by one. Their bodies falling from the air and shattering upon the ground. Nana, Snow, Erin, and Elder Arya were cornered, trying to fight their way to me. But they wouldn't reach me in time. Hope was disappearing. Dread began to take over. Panic raced through my mind. This could be the end.

Child, a soothing voice entered into my mind, *it is not the end.* A woman. *Enter into the veil, child, enter.* Her voice commanded and I obeyed. Closing my eyes, I tapped into my link, entering into the veil. The world was doused in magic around me. Shimmers of it dancing through the air. *Allow me to aid you, Willow.* Suddenly, I felt this power come over my body. Strength radiated within my very bones. Magic seared through my veins, pulsating and racing. A fiery burn of magic dwelled inside me, glowing brighter and brighter, engulfing my being.

The Exorcist's face no longer held a smirk, but wide eyes and a gaping mouth appeared on their face. The magic within me was howling to be set free, and set it free I would. Opening my mouth, a shout of power escaped. A surge of magic exploded from my being. A blast of light enveloped me, sending the Exorcist flying across the room.

Win this battle, child. Win. The woman's voice danced about my mind. So musical it was and so... familiar it sounded. Who was she?

"Willow!" Snow rushed to my side but stopped in her tracks, a gasp escaped her, "Willow..."

"What? What is it?"

Her hand trembled as it covered her mouth, "Your mark, your eyes."

"What about them?"

Elder Arya rushed over and she too, let out a gasp. "They're white, *glowing*." She said in awe.

"What?" I said with disbelief.

"And how did you do that? That magic?" The elder questioned me.

Snow helped me to stand, "I don't know. I just heard this voice..."

Before I could finish, Elder Arya whispered, "The Goddess."

"You mean, the Goddess spoke to *me*?" I could hardly believe it. She had spoken to me and saved my life.

"No one has spoken or seen her since the day she told the witches of the prophet child, five hundred years ago." Elder Arya said.

A roar sounded through the room, the last remaining stone

guardian had fallen. Its body shattered before our feet, scattering across the marble floor. Now, it was five against a hundred. More would join the battle soon. What chance did we stand against the Exorcist? Just our small group? The odds were against us.

The Exorcist circled us from above, watching. Their palms glowed but no attacks unleashed from them. I searched them, searching for my Exorcist. My eyes landed upon one, their hood covered their face, but their hands did not glow. Elrick. He was here, but not fighting. Staying in the background. My heart thumped as I continued to stare at him.

Claps sounded from far across the room. A man, bald with a cross tattooed across his scalp, entered into the room. Wisps of white hair grew from the sides of his head. His white robe swept across the floor behind him. Those ghostly eyes landed upon me, wrinkles formed around them, like crow's feet spanning from the corner of his eyes to the end of his bushy brows. A malicious smile formed upon his thin lips. His aged, veiny hands clasped together, "Ah, a pleasure to finally meet the prophet child." His voice sent a chill along my spine. "I knew you would come, Willow." His voice was hollow, ghostly.

Swallowing my fear, I straightened myself, "Where are my parents?" I demanded.

He raised a white brow, "Demanding things from me already? But we've only just met. Let's get to know one another first."

"There's nothing I want to know about you. I *want* my parents, *now*."

The Priest shook his head. "You must not realize where you are and who you are surrounded by." He raised a veiny hand into the air, "Grab her."

Two Exorcist launched from the air toward me. As Nana, Elder Arya, Snow, and Erin tried to protect me, they as well were grabbed by the enemy. The Exorcists that grabbed us, did not have glowing hands. Two of them had a hold on me, grasping both of my arms and knocking me down onto my knees. The Priest took a step toward me. Those ghostly eyes stared me down.

He knelt before me, his deathly cold hand grabbed my chin. "You are foolish to come here, brave, but foolish." He nodded his head to my captured group, "And only bringing four other witches with you was *foolish*. Did you honestly think that you five would stand a chance against us? Entering into the home of the Exorcists?" His face drew closer to mine. "Today, marks the end of the witches, thanks to your foolishness." A wicked smile formed upon his lips. "Such a pleasure it is to kill to prophet child."

He gave a nod to the Exorcists holding me. One of them grabbed a handful of my hair and jerked my head back. A yelp of pain sounded from me. The Priest chuckled as he stood behind me, towering over me. I was forced to stare into his eyes, "The end has come, for all witches. We have won and *you* have lost." The crosses tattooed onto his hands began to glow, emanating a holy light.

Fear claimed me. A cold sweat dripped down my spine. My body trembled. I fought against the Exorcists hold, trying to break free but to no avail. The Priest's hands crept closer and closer to my head. "Please…" I begged for my life.

A wicked grin crossed his lips, "Goodbye, Willow."

My eyes grew wide. It was over. We had lost. All of the witches' magic would be gone because *I* had failed. Those glowing hands were so close to me, heat radiated from the palms of his hands. My body was paralyzed with fear. Sweat dripped down my brow. I closed my eyes, accepting the end.

Then, a shout sounded through the room. My arms were set free as the Exorcists released their hold on me. Getting to my feet, I watched as Elder Esmerelda stormed into the cathedral, unleashing magical attacks through the room. Lightning and fire crackled through the room, knocking down enemies from the air.

While she vanquished enemies, I searched the room for the Priest. Hurriedly, he rushed from the room down a narrow hallway. Grabbing Snow and Erin's attentions, we followed after the Priest. Leaving Nana, Elder Arya, and Elder Esmerelda to finish off the Exorcists. Down we chased the Priest through the hall, his white robes rippling through the air behind him. Sharply, he turned a corner down another long hallway.

"Where is he going?" Snow asked breathlessly.

"Hopefully, to where my parents are."

At the end of the hall was a tall wooden door, the Priest thrust it open and disappeared behind it. Pushing myself to run faster, I barged through the door and found myself inside what appeared to be a dungeon. The smell of mildew wafted into the air. Cages lined along the walls. The metal bars were partially rusted. The Priest stood at the end of the room, a woman standing in front of him, her head hung low, her brown hair draped over her face. His hand glowed and was aimed at her head.

"You think you have won?" His voice echoed through the room. "You haven't! It is far from over, prophet."

The woman moaned and lifted her head. My breath was caught in my throat. My heart felt like it had stopped. My hands trembled. Her auburn eyes took in the sight of me, surprise and fear filled her beautiful face. "Willow..." Her lips whispered.

"Mom..." I took a shaking step forward. "Let her go."

The Priest shook his head, "I'm leaving here alive, with her. Or she dies." His glowing hand drew closer to my mother, "So, what will it be, Willow?"

Before I could say anything, my mother spoke, "Willow, don't let him go free."

I shook my head, tears burning in my eyes, "I can't stop him or he'll hurt you."

"My life does not matter. The fate of all witches is on your shoulders. Sacrificing one for the sake of everyone else is what must happen."

My knees buckled beneath me. The palms of my hands covered my eyes, "No!" Tears streamed down my cheeks. How could this be happening? My body shook.

Laughter echoed around me, sounding into my ears. "Weak, that is what you are, Willow." The priest said, "Now, this is goodbye until we meet again."

The Priest leapt into the air and flew through a colored window. Glass shattered across the floor, colorful pieces scattered around. My body lunged forward, *"Mom!"* My voice cried out desperately. I rushed toward the window but my feet slipped on the broken glass. Down I fell, the sharp pieces bit into my skin causing me to bleed. I lay in a heap on the floor, a heap of self-pity. Tears splashed onto the floor. "Mom…" She was here and then she was gone. In an instant, in a blink of an eye. What would the Priest do to her?

"Willow." Snow knelt beside me, "I think you might want to see this." She offered her hand to me.

Glancing at her waiting hand, I slid my hand onto her palm. She helped me to stand. Pieces of glass fell from my body as I stood. They crunched beneath my feet as Snow led me toward a cell. There was a figure hunched down in the corner. Shackles were clasped around his wrists. The man's dark hair covered his face. The barred door creaked as Snow opened it. Stepping into the dark, damp cell, the man turned to face me. His emerald eyes wide as our gazes met.

"Willow?" His voice rasped.

"Dad." I knelt before him and tried to unlock the shackles that chained him to the wall.

Snow placed a hand on my shoulder, "Stand back." She told me. Stepping away from my father, she spoke to him, "Extend your arms and turn your face away." My father obeyed and turned away, stretching out his arms. Aiming her white wand at the shackles, she called upon her magic, *"Oh magic of mine, come forth and send a blast of light."* Just as she commanded, a blast of light shot forth from her wand and hit the shackles, braking them away from my father's wrists.

He stood, a free man. "Willow." He said my name once more.

I rushed over to my father and threw myself into his embrace. His arms tightened around me. Tears burned within my eyes again. At least one of my parents was safe and sound.

"We should head back to the others." Erin said.

Wiping away my tears, I nodded my head.

* * *

When we returned, we found that Nana, Elder Arya, and Elder Esmerelda finished off the Exorcists. My heart sank into my stomach. My eyes searched every corpse for the auburn eyed Exorcist, but he was nowhere to be found. Relief washed over me, perhaps he got away and he was hiding somewhere within the building.

Nana rushed over to us, her bun was a mess, wisps of grey escaped from it. Her clothes were disheveled. "Where is she? Where is Lucinda?" She asked panicked.

My father and I exchanged sorrowful glances. "The Priest took her." I said.

Nana hung her head, "Not my daughter." Her voice cracked.

Stepping toward her, I wrapped my arms around my grandmother. "I'm sorry. I couldn't do anything."

Her hand patted my back, "It's not your fault, Willow." Stepping back, her aged hand cupped around my cheek, "You tried to save her, Willow. You did your best."

I shook my head, "If I did my best, she would be here with us."

The sound of someone clearing their throat interrupted our conversation. Elder Esmerelda stood behind Nana, her arms crossed over her chest, an eyebrow raised. Nana turned to face the elder woman. "How did you know we were here?"

"One of the gargoyles told me that a group of five took half of the stone guardians and headed east." Esmerelda answered with a scowl.

"Then I thank you, for your help."

"I'm not finished here." Her eyes narrowed upon me as she drew forth her wand. "There's one last thing I must take care of before we leave." She took a step toward me.

Nana moved to stand in front of me, her hand tightly grasped the handle of her wand, "What do you mean?"

The elder's eyes were still locked with mine, "You know what must be done." Her voice was low, coated with bitterness.

"You will not lay a hand on my granddaughter." Nana's voice sounded with warning.

"We cannot risk our magic, Anora. He was too close to destroying us tonight. Too close. We cannot allow that to happen again."

"Killing her will solve nothing, Esmerelda! She is the key to ending this war!" Nana's voice rose with anger.

The elder woman snapped her attention away from me and glared at my grandmother, "Don't you see? If we end her now the Exorcists won't be after us any longer." She jabbed her wand in my direction, "They're after her! The prophet!"

Nana shook her head, "You don't see that even if you killed Willow, the Exorcists will still hunt you down, one by one."

"Even so, we won't be under threat of our magic being taken from us." Esmerelda advanced forward.

Nana shoved me behind her, "I won't let you harm my granddaughter."

The elder raised a brow, "You won't? Then I guess I'll have to kill you as well, Anora."

"Nana…"

She peered over her shoulder, "I love you, Willow. Now

leave this place."

Suddenly, lightning stormed toward my grandmother, "Nana look out!" I cried.

Nana matched Esmerelda's attack. Their magic collided. Lightning and fire dancing together. Crackles and embers sounded and scattered about the room. Heat radiated from Nana's magic, from the flames. Her feet began to slide across the ground. Grasping ahold of her wand with both hands, she thrusted her wand to the side, causing their magic to slam into the wall. The lightning and fire blasted through the white marble, bits of debris flew into the air. The building moaned. Again, Esmerelda attacked. Another burst of lightning. White light flashed within the room as Nana summoned lightning as well. A blast of wind blew our way as their magic collided once more. Dust flew into my eyes, throwing up my arms, I shielded myself from the debris. The room was filled with magic. Sparks of it danced within the air.

"Get Willow out of here, *now*!" Nana commanded.

My father grasped ahold of my arm as he tried to tug me away from the dueling witches. Yanking free of his grasp, I argued, "We can't leave her here! We can't let her fight alone!"

"We have too." He tried to reach for me again, but I stopped him.

Calling upon my magic a barrier draped around me. A wall of wind. My father tried to reach me but to no avail. "We have to leave."

Debris slammed into my barrier, chucks of marble falling through the air. Gazing up, a massive hole had been blasted through the ceiling. The building moaned again. This place would collapse, soon. Turning to my father, I said, "Go! I'll get Nana and meet you outside, make sure the others get out safely, please."

My father let out a sigh of defeat. "Be safe, my daughter." With that, he ran off. Making sure that Elder Arya, Snow, and

Erin made it out safely.

Calling back my magic, I turned to face the still dueling witches. Wind and water swirled about and slammed into one another, drawing back and attacking again and again. Another moan and more pieces fell from the ceiling, the wall. "This place is falling apart! We have to leave!" I called out to them, my voice trying to reach them but they did not listen. Drawing forth my wand, I aimed it at the elder woman.

Esmerelda caught sight of me. Quickly she summoned upon another form of magic, vines took root and erupted through the marble floor. They danced around my grandmother and caught her in their earthly trap. Her wand was knocked from her hand. It fell to the floor.

Desperate to save Nana, I called upon my magic, *"Oh the most striking force, lightning this form of nature, I summon forth!"*

Lightning roared angrily from my wand as my emotions fueled it. It danced and thundered across the room toward the elder woman. Seeing my attack, she quickly summoned a barrier. My magic slammed into the wall of wind, the lightning ricocheting through the room. It blasted through walls and the ceiling. More and more of the building began to fall.

Rushing toward the barrier, I slammed my fist against it. "Please! Spare her!" I cried as she advanced toward my still trapped grandmother. "We have to leave! This place is falling apart! Please!" Tears swelled within my eyes.

The elder woman ignored my cries as she aimed her wand at my grandmother's chest, her heart. "I was always stronger than you, Anora."

Nana matched the woman's gaze, "But you'll never be stronger than Willow."

"Goodbye, Anora." The tip of her wand ignited with lightning.

My fists pounded against the barrier, *"No! Please, no!"*

Then, the lightning met with my grandmother's body. She convulsed. Her limbs twitching. Her eyes rolled into the back of her head. *"Nana!"* I cried out with heartache.

Her head slumped, her limbs went limp. The vines released their hold on my grandmother and her body slumped to the ground. "No…" My knees buckled beneath me. Down I fell. My hand clasped over my chest as my heart began to shatter piece by broken piece. Pain swelled within me, tightening my chest. It was hard to breathe. My vision was blurry. My mind a whirlwind of emotions and thoughts.

Nana was dead.

A scream clawed at my throat, begging to be released. My voice echoed around the room, loud and ear piercing. And with that scream the rest of my heart turned to dust. My grandmother was dead. Gone from this world. The woman who took care of me my entire life. Who raised me as her own daughter. And now, she would no longer be in my life. A pit of hollowness opened inside me. A pit of despair.

Glancing up, my eyes met with the elder woman's, the traitor, the *murderer*. She strode toward me, wand aimed at me. "And now, it is your turn, *prophet*."

The urge to survive had died along with my grandmother. My will to live vanished. I had failed trying to save my mother and now my grandmother was dead. Perhaps, there truly was no point in me remaining here. If Esmerelda ended me now, then the threat to the witches would no longer exist. No longer would their magic be threatened. And as long as I lived, it would always be threatened. Leaning my head down, I gave in. I gave up the fight.

Around us, the building moaned. The walls crumbled apart. The ceiling caving in, raining down on us. "This is the end, for us both." The elder said as she gazed upward toward the large chandelier that was falling down on us. "Our time has come." She closed her eyes, as did I. We waited for death to become us.

Time had slowed. Death took its sweet time reaching us. It was taunting me, mocking me. It whispered around me, filtering through my ears. Death sang its lullaby of a slumber I would never wake from. My time had come. Opening my eyes, I watched as the chandelier fell dangerously close. If I tried to run now, there would be no escaping my fate. It was too late to flee.

Then, a flash of white obscured my vision. Something slammed into my body, something tightened around me. I was flying across the room. The chandelier fell, crushing Elder Esmerelda. The glass sang as it shattered upon the floor. Then, along with the chandelier, the rest of the ceiling came crashing down. Pieces of marble rained from the building, landing upon the ground.

And just as I left the cathedral, the remainder of it fell down to the earth. Its beautiful, eerie marble structure lay in ruin. Thick dust wafted into the air, almost blinding me. My body landed upon the ground and I felt the presence of another hovering over me. An Exorcist loomed above me, their white hood covering their face. Part of me whispered not to fear them, and I listened. My hands pushed away the hood and I was drowning in a sea of auburn.

"Elrick…" My voice faintly whispered.

My Exorcist had saved me. "Willow." He spoke my name breathlessly. "Are you hurt?"

Then, I was reminded of my grandmother. Tears burned in my eyes. "She's gone."

Elrick's arms wrapped around my body, pulling me into his lap. "I'm sorry." He whispered into my ear as his hand stroked through my tangled hair.

I sobbed into his chest, my hands clutching his white robe. "She's gone…" Was all I could say.

Peering over his shoulder, I saw my father, Snow, Erin, and Elder Arya standing a few feet away. Their eyes were fixed upon me wrapped in the Exorcist's embrace. Confusion danced across their faces. None of them dared venture closer. Their gazes then moved to gaze upon the ruined cathedral, taking in the sight of the once home of the Exorcists.

Rising from the ground, Elrick and I approached the group of people. Each of them, except my father, aimed their wand toward the Exorcist beside me. Standing in front of him, I blocked him from any attacks. "He's with us." I spoke. "He won't hurt anyone of you."

"How can you be so sure?" Erin questioned.

Stepping aside, I grasped Elrick's had in mine. "Because," I found myself fumbling for the words to say. "Tonight, he saved my life when I never asked to be saved. He could have let me die in that building, but he didn't. He saved me."

Elder Arya raised a brow as she stared at our clasped hands, "How long?"

Meeting her gaze, I knew what she was asking. "Since I arrived at the council hall."

She nodded her head and dismissed the subject. "Where's your grandmother?" Before I could answer, she glanced at the ruined building and pieced the puzzle together. "I'm sorry for your loss, Willow."

My hand formed into a fist over my chest where the burning pain engulfed my heart. Elrick squeezed my hand gently, offering me comfort, telling me that he was here for me.

"Now what do we do?" Erin asked.

Our group turned and faced the ruined home of the Exorcists. Elder Arya answered her brother. "Now, the war has truly begun."

Made in the USA
Lexington, KY
02 November 2016